Matecumbe

UNIVERSITY PRESS OF FLORIDA

Florida A&M University, Tallahassee
Florida Atlantic University, Boca Raton
Florida Gulf Coast University, Ft. Myers
Florida International University, Miami
Florida State University, Tallahassee
New College of Florida, Sarasota
University of Central Florida, Orlando
University of Florida, Gainesville
University of North Florida, Jacksonville
University of South Florida, Tampa
University of West Florida, Pensacola

University Press of Florida

Gainesville · Tallahassee · Tampa · Boca Raton · Pensacola · Orlando · Miami · Jacksonville · Ft. Myers · Sarasota

Matecumbe

James A. Michener

Afterword by Joe Avenick

Copyright 2007 by Joe Avenick

Cover photograph by Perry Hodies III

Printed in the United States of America on recycled, acid-free paper

12 11 10 09 08 07   6 5 4 3 2 1

Library of Congress Cataloging-in-Publication Data

Michener, James A. (James Albert), 1907–1997.

Matecumbe / James A. Michener ; afterword by Joe Avenick.

p. cm.

ISBN 978-0-8130-3152-1 (acid-free paper)

1. Florida Keys (Fla.)—Fiction. I. Title.

PS3525.I19M38 2007

813'.54—dc22   2007005304

The University Press of Florida is the scholarly publishing agency for the State University System of Florida, comprising Florida A&M University, Florida Atlantic University, Florida Gulf Coast University, Florida International University, Florida State University, New College of Florida, University of Central Florida, University of Florida, University of North Florida, University of South Florida, and University of West Florida.

University Press of Florida

15 Northwest 15th Street

Gainesville, FL 32611-2079

http://www.upf.com

Matecumbe

Chapter 1

Mary Ann Catherine Mays was born in Pennsylvania and spent most of her childhood living on a small chicken farm just outside Pottstown. Life was hard on the farm. There were always chores to do—feed to scatter, chicken coops to clean. She always felt sorry for the chickens and their short, penned-in existence. She was attending St. Aloysius High and had almost completed her sophomore year when she decided to leave school and get married to her dad's auto mechanic. A life of cars and garages seemed so much more exciting than chickens.

Mary Ann and Donald Pienta had four children, all girls. But immediately after their eighth anniversary, the marriage was over. Donald had disappeared—leaving Mary Ann to care for the children.

Despite severe economic hardship, Mary Ann kept the family together. After all, she was used to dealing with adversity since her childhood. She'd work odd jobs, often two or three at the same time. Occasionally, she'd get help with the bill paying from a scattering of local relatives.

Whenever her daughters would ask the inevitable question, Mary Ann would say: "We're not poor, we're just low income. Poor people don't have homes. They live in cars or in barns with the farm animals. We have an apartment."

Medical bills constituted the most frightening of Mary Ann's expenses. For whenever Melissa, Susan, Denise, or Annie would get ill unexpectedly, all previously designed budgets had to be scuttled. The girls' asthmatic conditions called for constant monitoring.

"I'll barter with your doctor," Mary Ann told her oldest, when the damp-eyed teenager expressed worry about the cost of an emergency room visit. "Your grandmom and grandpop still have lots of chickens."

As she walked along the beachfront of the Seascaper Resort Motel, Melissa Tomlinson was relieved that no one could see the tears that she quickly wiped from her cheeks. It was a spontaneous cry, born from pleasant memories.

She had come to the Seascaper to rejuvenate her life, to put back some semblance of mental order to a psyche that had been shredded to nothingness as a result of the recent divorce.

The Seascaper had been friendly to her in the past, and so had the little town in the Florida Keys—Islamorada—on whose beaches she now walked.

The word "Islamorada" is literally translated from the Spanish as "Purple Island." This is due, no doubt, to the wild and colorful bougainvillea that grow everywhere, as if they were the ever-present springtime dandelions that cover farmlands and suburban lawns alike in her native Pennsylvania.

The tiny town of Islamorada, covering Upper Matecumbe Key, lies about halfway between Miami and Key West. The entire island is less than a mile wide, and from Route 1, the only highway, you can see the sparkling waters of the Gulf of Mexico on one side and the Atlantic Ocean on the other.

Thousands of years ago, there were no Florida Keys. When dinosaurs roamed the mainland, these islands were hidden under the ocean. But like buried treasure, they rose from beneath the swells, gem-like, to add a tiara of sparkling beauty to the mass of warm-weather vegetation that would come to be known as Florida.

Melissa stopped walking when she reached the easternmost point of the Seascaper's grounds, where the sandy surface ended abruptly, and a line of large black rocks, forming a jetty, separated her from the sea.

She looked briefly over her shoulder at the setting sun, its orange glow quickly disappearing into what seemed to be the far end of the ocean. This powerful spectacle always seemed to evoke an increase in her visual vocabulary.

"I hope," she told herself, "that this will not be symbolic of the rest of my days. I am determined that all the sunshine in my life will not be limited to my past." For after thirteen years as a faithful wife, Melissa was recently divorced from Brady Tomlinson, a tenured English teacher at the University of Pennsylvania. They had been college sweethearts who'd married two weeks after graduation—the June wedding that Melissa had always dreamed she'd have. Now, suddenly, Brady had been excised forever from her life—with the swiftness of a sharp-edged sword cutting down flowers in full bloom.

The week lying ahead of her would mark Melissa's first vacation without Brady since she was a teenager. There was no hope of reviving their relationship. It would be like trying to calm a tiger in the rain.

"Losing Brady was like losing a pet," Melissa had told Cammie, her best friend and fellow reference librarian. "It was just like when the veterinarian advised me to have Pops, my cat, put to sleep. That's the feeling I had when I signed the first of the divorce papers."

Cammie, who was Melissa's confidante as well as her co-worker in a Philadelphia library, had never been married.

"At least now we can go to the singles bars together," Melissa had laughed. "Being six years younger than me, though, you'll probably get the best of what's left out there."

Before she could even begin to embark with Cammie on what she feared would probably be a difficult manhunt, Melissa wanted to return, alone, to Islamorada, which was, without a doubt, her most favorite place in the world. Though she had traveled extensively with Brady throughout the most popular of Europe's tourist centers—in England, France, Italy, and Greece—her visits to Islamorada generated the most cherished memories.

In fact, Melissa had journeyed to Islamorada even before she'd met Brady. During the spring vacation of her freshman year in college, she and three of her dormitory sisters had driven off to Islamorada on a day trip from their lodgings in Fort Lauderdale. She had come to escape then, too. The motel they were staying at in Fort Lauderdale was filled with a fraternity from the University of Michigan, which was fun at first. But two nights into their stay the police raided a party the boys were having in one of their rooms, and the whole gang was taken down to the local police station where they were all forced to spend the night. A calming junket to Islamorada was just what their frightened spirits needed before returning to college.

And with Brady, Melissa had come often to this ever-sunny, tropical isle. She suspected, however, that she enjoyed this peaceful hideaway much more than Brady did. The solitude of the island was at the core of its appeal to Melissa, and at this crucial juncture in her life, she knew that Islamorada would allow her some precious time to think. Melissa realized that she needed to be free from the distractions of the working world in order to refresh her battered soul.

She also wanted to be able to return home from this eight-day island vacation as an invigorated woman—ready to re-pursue her life's dual goals of continued success as a reference librarian and happiness as a wife—the wife of an as-yet-unknown man who would love her for the remainder of their years together.

"The December sunshine in Florida will help my looks, too," Melissa admitted. "I have a sexy figure, and I'm still thin—thanks to exercise, I guess. But a suntan always makes my face look just a trifle younger. And the younger I look, the younger the guys will be who'll show an interest in me. I don't want to get involved with a teenager, certainly, but I don't want to attract the graybeards either."

Melissa contented herself with the knowledge that she had always been a good-looking woman. Not as ravishing perhaps as the typical nighttime soap opera star, but close enough.

With deep-set brown eyes and pixie-like movements, despite her average height, Melissa Pienta had broken more than a few hearts in high school and college. Although she wasn't as young and as fresh-faced as Cammie, she was far from old. And to her credit, she exuded the class of a mature, well-informed woman. It was her alert mind, and perhaps her high IQ, she concluded, that had convinced the scholarly Brady, many years ago, to ask for her hand in marriage.

Melissa knew that although Brady had an ultra-skinny, super-slight build, this absence of muscles did not detract from his being considered a handsome catch. His ready wit and the tender things he'd always say to her more than made up for his lack of brawn.

Unfortunately, just as he would always seem to become bored slightly with Islamorada after a few days of beach, water, and sun, Brady had, over the last few years, become bored with his Melissa.

"The excitement is gone from our marriage," he'd told her, bluntly.

This boredom label that Brady had bestowed on her was the deepest hurt for Melissa. It was far from a kind comment, especially since Brady was keenly aware of Melissa's constant battles with self-confidence.

Now he was involved with a bond trader on the New York Stock Exchange who also kept a weekend escape house outside of New Hope, Pennsylvania. I'm sure that she is anything but boring, Melissa thought to herself when the vision of Brady's new love entered her mind.

With Brady gone, Melissa wondered what the next man in her life would look like—if there were to be a next man.

The sun had completely disappeared from the sky by the time Melissa had walked back to the tiny office of the Seascaper.

The town of Islamorada, as well as this beachfront motel, hadn't changed much in the six years since she'd last visited. The general store with real pickle barrels was still a fixture, but it had competition now in the form of an ever-busy convenience store. A sprawling, three-story hotel and a drive-through hamburger emporium were also new. The town, though, if you could erase all traces of ocean, could pass for a sparsely populated hillside hamlet somewhere deep in West Virginia's coal country—such were the buildings that sat alongside the oft-deserted main highway.

The rustic post office, the lone gas station, and the trailer park with the neon sign all flashed a time in history when America spun more to 45 R.P.M. than to chic corporate culture.

Melissa was amused more than annoyed when she saw that the sign she'd read earlier was still posted on the door to the Seascaper's office.

—DON'T BE DOUR
BE BACK IN ONE HOUR
OUT FISHING FOR DINNER—

Typical of this part of the world, Melissa thought. People in the Keys may be slackers, but they're poetic slackers. They always seem to give business a backseat to the pleasures of everyday living.

Florida, she reasoned, could be just as laid back as California claims to be, but much more earthy.

All told, it had been an hour since she'd arrived here by rental car after flying non-stop from Philadelphia to Miami. The eighty-mile drive from the airport to Islamorada had tired her slightly, and Melissa wondered how much longer it would be before she could check in and take a much-needed, refreshing shower.

But resigned now to an even further wait, thanks to the desk clerk's fishing expedition, she sat on the fender of her car for what turned into yet another half hour. Finally, after putting her now useless sunglasses on the car's dashboard, Melissa decided to walk along the beach toward the eastern end of the Seascaper complex.

Although the weather was far from cold, the breezes from the Caribbean rippled coolly and crisply through the palm trees, whipping the giant fronds into a hushed tune that sounded like rain but wasn't.

Melissa's immediate goal was the pier that jutted out some two hundred feet from the beach toward the general direction of Cuba. She had fished on this pier with Brady, catching tiny, pastel-striped relatives of sea bass known as cowfish. The water in Islamorada was so clear that during daylight hours she remembered being able to look straight through to the bottom, watching the colorful underwater life swim by and seeing an occasional fish chance a nibble on a baited hook.

Nighttime, too, offered its sensual rewards. An evening walk to the end of the pier always seemed to put Melissa into oneness with nature. She guessed it was because she was standing, and breathing, in a spot where she shouldn't be—two hundred feet offshore and, during high tide, only inches over the water line. Here, the moonlight brightening an ocean horizon was complemented by the sound of tiny, rippling waves.

It wasn't until she had reached the end of the pier and was staring toward clouds and stars that Melissa realized how dark it really was. She might not have found the pier at all if she hadn't known, in advance, where to look for it. The light-starved sky was certainly no help.

"Didn't I see small, round lights out here last time?" she asked herself. "I seem to remember little yellow bulbs attached to the upper railings."

Suddenly, Melissa's attention was given to the sound of a motorboat. And though her eyes were getting accustomed to the dark, she could not see a craft of any size near the pier.

While the motor's howl continued to increase at an alarming rate, she scanned in all directions, flipping her head from side-to-side as if it were the periscope of a submarine, but she could see nothing. Melissa was holding onto the railing in fright now, which would be to her benefit. The roaring sound had become unbearably loud.

She saw it an instant before it crashed into the center of the pier, halfway between her and the beach. The boat, like the pier, had no lights. It was a speedboat, about twenty feet long.

If Melissa hadn't been gripping the railing, the force of the impact would have thrown her into the water. Still, the crash knocked her onto the flooring of the pier, toward the opposite railing some four feet away.

As she lay there, seemingly unharmed except for a wood-scraped left elbow, she saw what remained of the speedboat go up in flames.

Righting herself, she watched in horror as the burning boat cut out her only path back to shore.

Within seconds, the flames were shooting high into the air, illuminating the shoreline. Looking back toward the Seascaper, Melissa could tell that a small crowd had now begun to gather on the beach.

"Help! Help!" Melissa screamed, over and over, waving her arms. She stopped only when she realized she had been spotted, for some of those on shore were pointing back to her while others waved in recognition.

After about fifteen additional minutes of panic, worrying about the burning wood between her and safety and about whether the speedboat would explode, Melissa sighed in relief as she saw a rescue boat begin to approach. It looked like an abbreviated tugboat, wide and sturdy, complete with blinking red lights and a huge floodlight near the bow. At the same time, on the opposite side of the pier, a small fireboat appeared, hosing water on the flames.

There was only one passenger in the rescue boat, a tall man who may have seemed taller because he was standing behind a small steering wheel, which he maneuvered in front of him at thigh level. He was wearing a policeman's jacket and slacks, a gun, and a grayish, western style hat with a huge star just above the brim. She had harbored a fear of policemen, especially southern policemen, since her college experience in Fort Lauderdale. But now, he was as welcome a sight to Melissa as John Wayne was to many a cinematic damsel. Instead of a white stallion, though, he had driven up at the helm of a police boat that seemed as brightly decorated as a Christmas tree.

"You all right, ma'am?" he queried, extending his arm, gently, to help her on board.

Melissa accepted the blanket he quickly offered, which she used to cover her now shivering shoulders. She was thankful that she was still wearing the warm winter suit she'd put on in Philadelphia for the plane ride south.

Melissa stared upward at his profile as he pointed the boat back toward land. His well-chiseled features, highlighted by the dying blaze, suggested a tough man, but his voice was compassionate.

"Were you a passenger on the boat that crashed, ma'am?" John Wayne asked her.

"No," Melissa countered. "I'm Melissa Tomlinson. I'm a guest at the Seascaper."

Officer Joe Carlton, as he'd soon introduced himself, docked the rescue boat and then drove Melissa to a medical center on the other side of town. She couldn't help but notice the sparkling blue eyes of her rescuer when, in the emergency room, he smiled and said he'd wait for her while a doctor tended to her bruised elbow.

A friendly, slightly overweight physician checked her X-rays and told Melissa that she had no broken bones.

While she sat, feeling vulnerable, Melissa remembered her long-ago trips to doctors' offices for treatment of her childhood asthma. On more than one occasion, Melissa's mom would complain about a doctor being inattentive or in a hurry to finish a consultation.

Her mother was always doing verbal battle with the doctors who cared for Melissa and her sisters. Melissa remembered that her mom even considered writing a book called PATIENT OR PERSON—"about doctors who don't listen sympathetically because they're in a hurry to receive their money."

After being treated and bandaged, and pronounced fit except for a few scratches, Melissa was back in Officer Carlton's car, headed again for the Seascaper.

The calming combination of her slowly ebbing fright and the commanding presence of her handsome rescuer left Melissa temporarily mute. As well, an occasional drone from the vehicle's siren seemed to discourage conversation.

"God, he's good-looking," she told herself. "He seems to be about my age, too."

Despite her misgivings about policemen, her initial attraction to Officer Carlton was so strong that Melissa found herself wishing she could suddenly transform herself into a pert, cheerful debutante—and shed the disheveled, physically drained image she no doubt projected.

"When you rescued me, what made you ask if I were on the boat, Detective Carlton?" Melissa inquired, tentatively, addressing him with an incorrect title.

"Marijuana," he answered, in what seemed like an affected southern drawl. "But just call me Joe. Everyone in Islamorada calls me Joe.

"By the way, I was just informed by police radio that the two fellows who were on that speedboat are dead. Their bodies were found a few minutes ago. Earlier, while you were being rescued, several bales of marijuana floated ashore. We assume that they flew out of the boat on impact. So, my original suspicion was that the impact also threw you—from the boat to the pier.

"I guess you'd like to be left off at the Seascaper office, so you can pick up your key," Joe continued.

"Why, yes, but how did you . . ."

"I talked with the Seascaper folks while you were in the X-ray room. They told me you didn't check in yet. But you are Melissa Tomlinson, like you said you were, from Philadelphia, Pennsylvania. My Uncle Steve lives not far from Philly."

"Oh, where?"

"Somerdale, New Jersey. Nice little town, but too cold for me this time of year.

"I'll check up on you tomorrow, to see how you are," Joe nodded, as he turned off his cruiser's flashing light long enough to say good-bye.

"It probably won't be easy for you, Ms. Tomlinson, but try to get some rest."

Chapter 2

The oftentimes-boring job she held as a secretary at the electric company paid most of her bills, but Mary Ann had to fight hard to stretch every penny. A typical weekday lunch consisted of coffee and a package of crackers—followed by a window-shopping stroll through the center of Pottstown.

At Christmas time one year, Mary Ann sold her ancient kitchen table ("It's almost an antique," she told the buyer) so she'd have enough money to buy presents that the girls asked for. After the holiday season, the cold of winter always seemed endless. She worried constantly about the heating bill and keeping her girls warm.

Luckily, Mary Ann was good at finding money. By keeping her eyes focused downward whenever she walked on sidewalks or crossed streets, she was able to spot coins that had fallen from pockets or purses. She picked up pennies and nickels totaling about two or three dollars a month. Mary Ann even trained her girls to look for money in the coin-return slots of public telephones and vending machines. The girls found quarters and dimes mostly, and this total hovered at about eight dollars a month.

From the proceeds of her found money, Mary Ann would occasionally play a ten-cent "street number" with her neighborhood bookie. She never hit a jackpot.

From fall until early spring, she'd send the girls out to look for firewood. They'd pack the tiny kindling, branches, and broken pieces into bundles and sell them to neighbors. Their best firewood customer, however, gave up on the Pienta family's haphazard product when he moved and bought an impressive, 12-room house in the fashionable section of town.

"I'll just be using mahogany, oak, and white birch from now on," he told Mary Ann's children. "They look prettier on the woodpile, and they burn a lot longer in my fireplaces."

One of Mary Ann's biggest frustrations was not being able to get any of the big credit cards, even though she'd applied for a number of them. She heard the refusal reasons numerous times. "Your earnings are too low, your expenses are too high, and your husband once filed for bankruptcy."

One Saturday she found an expensive brown leather wallet right outside the confessional at church. It had a name monogrammed in small gold letters: "Paul Reynolds."

She was the last person left in the church outside of the priest who was still in the confessional, so she quickly slipped it inside her purse and ran from the church. After she had reached home, she found over $200 in the wallet. There was even a crisp new $50 bill. She had never seen a $50 bill before. Mary Ann sat and stared at the wallet for hours.

She knew she could use the money. Her work shoes were beyond resoling, and Melissa needed new medication for her asthma. From the quality of the wallet, it appeared that the owner certainly could afford to lose it and buy another one.

Still, she knew she couldn't keep it. Stray nickels and pennies were one thing, this was really stealing. She'd always made it through tough times before without resorting to dishonesty. There was no identification in the wallet other than the gold monogram, so, after exhaustive contemplation, she decided there was only one thing to do.

She reached for her coat and took the wallet back to the church. The doors were now locked, so, instead, she knocked with painful hesitation at the next-door rectory, a small older building where the pastor resided. She felt her heart beating quickly as she stood there, hearing nothing inside. Her eyes wandered upward, resting on a small cupola above the roof of this stone, stately structure. Two birds chirped over her head, then danced on the eaves, seeming to add a touch of poetry to the façade.

Pastor Stevens answered the door, and for a moment Mary Ann stood dumbfounded, unable to explain why she had rung the bell. Pastor Stevens saw her consternation, took her arm and said, "Come in, Mary Ann. What brings you out on such a cold night?"

Mary Ann took the wallet from her purse sheepishly and handed it to Pastor Stevens.

"I found this wallet earlier in the church, Father. And even though we can desperately use the money, I just can't keep it. It would be stealing, and I could never live with myself knowing I was reduced to that."

Pastor Stevens thanked Mary Ann for her honesty, and promised he wouldn't divulge her identity when he found the wallet's rightful owner.

⬧

Going to church was a Sunday morning ritual for Mary Ann and the girls. The wearing of hats, gloves, and innovative, homemade dresses always seemed extra special. After Mass one cool morning in early March, several weeks after the wallet episode, Mary Ann smiled politely as Father Stevens introduced her to a man named Paul Reynolds.

"A bank executive, Mary Ann," the priest emphasized. "Paul here might be able to help you get a credit card." Mary Ann's heart was pounding. She knew that Father Stevens would not betray her, but what was he up to?

Several minutes later, while Mary Ann and the girls were walking home, Paul Reynolds jogged up behind them, out of breath, to continue the earlier conversation.

"How about," he offered, "some coffee and a little brunch?"

Simultaneously, the girls cheered. Despite her rattled psyche, Mary Ann could not bear to disappoint the girls. After all, they were only going to face a modest lunch of hot dogs and beans at home. So she reluctantly said yes.

Afterwards, Mary Ann's youngest spoke of Reynolds as "the man with the calico mustache, orange, black, and gray, just like a cat might be."

⬧

Melissa's eyes popped open at about eight o'clock the next morning. And although her elbow did ache slightly from last night's misadventure, the warm Florida air proved to be a soothing tonic—not only for her physical state of health but also for her recently savaged, but silent, mental condition.

"It's always been so easy for me to relax in warmer weather," she told herself. "I have no doubt that these balmy breezes can wash away some of the pain from my divorce. I'll just forget the boat collision from last night and get on with my vacation. Who knows? Maybe some handsome stranger awaits me this week, among the smiling music of tiki bars and the controlled merriment of singles fun in the sun."

Melissa possessed scores of memories that had been evoked by warm weather. She and Brady had spent two weeks in sunny Athens a few years ago with a side excursion to see the ancient ruins and intricate mazes near Iráklion on the island of Crete. And the August prior, they had vacationed on the beaches of southern France. Memories always seemed richer and longer lasting when the experiences occurred in soothing summery weather, where she could commune much easier with nature.

Melissa flitted about her beachfront motel room at the Seascaper for over an hour—unpacking suitcases and organizing her wardrobe for the week—while dressed only in a sheer lace nightgown with matching panties—part of the entire new wardrobe of lingerie she had afforded herself when the final divorce papers were signed.

As she puttered, the sun outside was already warming the sand and the clear blue waters of the Gulf. When Melissa peeked through the curtains on the patio side of her room, she could see the scene of last night's tragedy. The remains of the speedboat had been removed, but the pier had been roped off from public access. A huge, fire-scarred gap sat between the two separated sections of the pier.

Apparently, the fire had continued to burn toward the far end, almost to the point where Melissa had been rescued. Seagulls and pelicans were now congregating on the abbreviated edge, wondering, perhaps, what had happened to the pier's fishermen, with whom they would usually share the morning catch.

After slipping into a pair of pink and blue slacks and a matching pink tee shirt, and applying just a trace of lipstick for some much needed color in her face, Melissa started to walk along the mile-and-one-half of adjacent beach. As she strolled past a group of date palm trees, she stopped to say hello to an egret, a tall, pure-white bird the size of a small flamingo. With their spindly, toothpick legs and long, retractable necks, these slow-walking birds appear to be vulnerable and flighty. Yet the egrets in Islamorada, Melissa remembered, were not so easily spooked. Most of the time they were so friendly that they'd walk right up to seaside sunbathers and seem to stand guard like faithful family dogs.

She promised "Snowy," as she called the bird, that she would be back later that afternoon with a tasty handout. Fish, preferably.

During her walk, Melissa snapped off a wild purple hibiscus, the stem of which she had tied onto a lock of her short, brown hair. Then, before long, she made her way over to the Seascaper's restaurant.

Fresh fruit, fresh orange juice, and the most delicious, honey-dipped biscuits she had ever tasted were what she recalled about breakfasts at the Seascaper. The mere act of thinking about food again whetted her appetite even more. The last meal she'd eaten had featured a dull, warmed over chunk of chicken breast—courtesy of yesterday afternoon's southbound airline.

At the Seascaper, Melissa was all ears as her waitress described how an island-wide power outage the night before had knocked out the lights on the pier. The speedboat smugglers then failed to see the structure in the resulting darkness.

"And I heard," the waitress continued, as Melissa listened, with a straight face, "that one of our guests was rescued from the edge of the pier—pulled into a police boat with her bikini on fire!"

Melissa also discovered, with a bit more reliability, that the desk clerk, who was supposed to be on duty when she had tried to check in, was forced to go hungry. Reportedly, he had caught a dinner-sized fish, just as his hand-written sign had prophesied, but he was unable to cook it once the power failure had rendered his electric stove inoperative. Undoubtedly, this clerk was no lover of sushi.

Soon, after sharing a polite laugh with the waitress and while waiting for her food to be served, Melissa started thinking about Joe—and whether he would, indeed, "check up" on her as he'd promised.

"It would be nice," she told herself, "if he would take more than a cop-talks-to-suspect interest in me."

Melissa wondered, though, exactly how she should react if Joe decided to pursue her romantically. She'd certainly need to get over her aversion to southern policemen. Besides, she had been removed from the dating game for such a long time now that she was uncertain of her woman-meets-man social skills.

Her mind skipped briefly to concerns about his marital status. Melissa was silently convincing herself that he wasn't married. The only positive hint in this direction was the absence of any wedding ring—which Melissa noticed last night. She knew, though, that married men do not always wear the rings. Some, especially those with roving eyes, choose not to bear the burden of such branding.

Being so far from her Philadelphia home, Melissa felt fairly secure that she couldn't embarrass herself either professionally or with her ultra-liberal, trendy acquaintances if she condescended, class-wise, to date a "Cop Named Joe." The value she always placed on "what other people think," however, made her uneasy.

Melissa had heard stories of well-educated women like herself who would vacation yearly in the Caribbean without their husbands. They would spend a lust-filled week playing in the sun with the young, native men before returning home as "faithful" wives. She knew that her staunch morals wouldn't permit her to go to that extreme, and she was thankful.

She finally convinced herself that although dating a policeman back home in Philadelphia might make her look sex-starved to her college educated co-workers, no harm would come of such a liaison over a thousand miles from her Philadelphia library and from her Philadelphia circle of friends.

There did remain one other problem, though.

"Damn it," she scowled, as she sipped her freshly squeezed orange juice. "I should have talked more at length with Cammie about the new wave sexual etiquette. If he's an eligible man, am I expected to make love to him right away, just because we're both unattached, or will my chances of catching him be better if I play hard to get? Has the long-established standard of no kiss until the third date turned into a mandatory third date in bed? Or do men just disappear now after only one or two celibate get-togethers? And what about AIDS? What am I supposed to do about that? Are women always supposed to be prepared with condoms? Does that make me look easy or smart?"

Melissa had little time to contemplate any answers to this quandary, for as soon as her papaya slices and biscuits arrived, so did Joe.

"Hi, there. Can I sit with you and buy us both some coffee?" he asked.

As soon as Melissa answered quickly in the affirmative, she smiled, almost blushing. And although Joe's sudden appearance came too close on the heels of thoughts she did not yet want to share with him, Melissa was immediately turned on by his presence.

In the daylight, he looked to be a slightly different person. Still handsome, with the same bedroom eyes, he seemed more normal without his "Smoky" hat. He was once again wearing a policeman's uniform, but Melissa could see his hair now, a curly brown with light strands of gray on the sideburns. He seemed more vigorous and less stilted than he had last night. She wondered what he would be like when not on duty, as if any policeman, married to the structure and discipline of his job, could ever be away from duty.

Melissa felt a strange comfort in sharing her table with this powerful-looking man whose smile radiated all the good things that a man could be. Seeing him again caused her whole body to glow. It was like walking into a warm room after an outdoor stroll on an icy evening.

Melissa told him that she felt just fine now and was hoping she could put last night behind her and complete her plans to stay in Islamorada for a week of sun and relaxation.

"How long will it take them to fix the pier?" she began.

"When I talked to Larry Basson, the owner of the Seascaper, early this morning," Joe related, "he told me he intended to hire a crew as soon as possible. He said he'd pay them whatever it takes to get the pier fixed in time for January and February, the heart of the winter season. It'll cost plenty to repair it in just two or three weeks, but the pier is one of the reasons that the Seascaper is so popular."

"I guess," Melissa informed, "that you know already what the waitress told me. The power outage last night knocked out the lights on the pier, and that's why the boat crashed into it."

"Oh, yes, and the lack of lights might result in an insurance payment delay for the Seascaper. Seems there's some question as to whether the electric company has some liability. But Basson said he'll fix the pier anyway and worry about insurance later."

Melissa felt relieved that "her" pier would once again be in operation, even though she wouldn't be able to walk on it any more during her current vacation.

Joe had already begun his second cup of coffee before he hit Melissa with the big news of the morning.

"We found out that the two guys on that boat were from Philadelphia, just like you," he stated, nonchalantly, without further comment. Joe paused for another sip just then, as if he were waiting to assess the truthfulness of Melissa's immediate reaction.

"What? . . . Where in Philadelphia? . . . What neighborhood are they from?"

"Both of them lived in the same building on Pine Street. I think the number was seventeen hundred and something. Is that anywhere near you?"

"No, not really. I live in a section called Logan. Pine Street is in downtown Philadelphia, what the natives call Center City. What were the names of those two men?"

"Baron Marshall and Jayson Harris," Joe recited, "two guys with police records for dealing in drugs. Marshall was thirty-eight years old, and Harris was thirty-two.

"I imagine," Joe continued, "that I would be derelict in my duty if I didn't ask you if you knew either of them."

"I don't understand."

"Well," Joe went on, seemingly embarrassed now, "the Monroe County detective that I talked to this morning speculated that you might have been waiting for them on the pier, that you were out there to signal them that it was safe to dock. And perhaps the three of you intended to load the bales of marijuana into your car."

"Are you serious? That rental car of mine is a hatchback. It doesn't have a trunk. It wouldn't even hold one bale of marijuana. And do I look like the type of woman," Melissa responded, raising her voice slightly, her eyes narrowing, "who would be involved with drugs? Of course I don't know those men. I never heard of either of them."

"Now just calm down, Miss Tomlinson. I certainly don't have any personal belief that you knew the two men. My gut feeling is that you were not a part of their operation, and I gave that opinion to the detective. Also, from the way you reacted just now, my law enforcement experience tells me I'm right—you didn't know the two men."

Shaken slightly, Melissa felt she was on the verge of being terribly upset. But she knew that she would have difficulty complaining as strongly as she may have desired. Joe's apologetic, sincere little speech in her defense couldn't be countered with too wild an outburst. She wondered, though, if she could ever achieve friendship with a man whose suspicious nature probably churned continually for twenty-four hours of every living day. Maybe her aversion to policemen was justified after all.

Melissa still wanted to defend herself, however, and she soon began to spew forth words for the sake of talking. Emotional release was replacing all traces of calm.

"First of all, don't call me 'Miss Tomlinson.' I dislike that as much as being called 'Hon' or 'Babe.' Since I'm no longer married, you can't really call me 'Mrs. Tomlinson,' so I'd appreciate a simple 'Melissa.' And I guess I should be thankful for your vote of confidence. I just wish I could prove to you somehow that I didn't know those two men."

After Joe made several additional reassuring remarks, Melissa seemed to regain her composure. She even contemplated, ever so daringly, that perhaps she should utter a tiny lie and tell Joe that she really did know the two men—just to be ornery—to see if he could find it in his heart to punish her.

"If naughty Melissa were ever to act like a bad girl," she whispered to her conscience, "Joe would be one of the few men she'd let give her the spanking she deserved."

"I'm here in Islamorada to try to relax this week, Joe," she told him. "But instead of being able to forget all about my divorce, I seem to be adding to my list of things to worry about. One part of me now is begging to get on a plane for Philadelphia as soon as possible."

"That's not necessary at all, Melissa," Joe responded, reaching to pay for both their checks with one of his credit cards. "Look, I'm satisfied that you're as uninvolved with the two dead men as you say you are. I'm willing to put up a 'Case Closed' sign as far as you're concerned. Just like with all the other tourists who come to Islamorada, my only concern now is that you enjoy yourself and tell your friends about what a great place this is to have a vacation. If you want, I'll walk out of your life right now. But before you say 'that's a good idea,' I do feel somewhat guilty about how upset you got when I asked you if you had known the two dead men.

"So," Joe concluded, and this time it was his turn to fight back a blush, "would you like to have dinner with me tonight? Aside from feeling I owe you something for getting your vacation off to a bad start, I've found I really do enjoy your company. And we won't talk business at all—I promise. We'll just be two unattached people having a fun evening together."

Unhesitatingly, Melissa agreed.

For the remainder of the day, while she sunned herself by the freshwater pool, swam a few laps in the saltwater pool, and fed bait-sized shrimp to the friendly egret, she thought of nothing but her upcoming date with "Joe The Cop," as she referred to him inwardly. Her overall impressions of Joe were positive. She knew, though, that it often took time, much time, before she could be sure that a prospective love interest didn't have a Jekyll and Hyde personality.

As she continued to contemplate her date, Melissa searched her memory but couldn't recall, even in high school, ever having gone out with a guy who had so many muscles.

"I think I've succeeded in getting what I was fantasizing about this morning," she told herself. "I just wish I could forget completely about that dreadful boat accident. But I can't help thinking that he just wants to keep an eye on me, to see if I'll slip and say something that'll lead him to think I knew the two dead drug dealers.

"However," Melissa concluded, as she ended her day in the sun and began to shower and prepare for the date, "I'll give big, handsome Joe the benefit of the doubt. Who knows? We may eventually live happily ever after—but it would have to be in a place somewhere other than Islamorada," she daydreamed, once again. "Though this is a great place to visit, it's much too far south of my professional ambitions."

While slipping into her lacy camisole, Melissa reasoned that if Joe weren't so attractive, or if he were a woman detective, she'd probably check out of her room at the Seascaper right away and drive straight to the airport in Miami.

Instead she looked admiringly at her reflection in the mirror. Her slight new sunburn glowed on her shoulders and neck, contrasting with the white sheerness of her camisole.

"Now I know what all of those other women mean," she reflected, "when they say they made the biggest mistakes of their lives by letting their brains follow their sex organs.

"Melissa the snob," she said, while looking in the bathroom mirror and giving herself a talking-to, "meet Melissa the common, average, everyday, boring woman."

Chapter 3

Shortly after the brunch came the first big dinner date. And since her romantic experiences had been limited to only a handful of suitors, Mary Ann feared that she wouldn't remember how to act while being courted by an eligible man. These feelings of insecurity were further compounded by her embarrassment that Paul's had been the wallet she had found in the church. Would he possibly be interested in her if he knew that she had almost stooped to stealing? She had, almost. But in the end she did the right thing and returned the wallet. There was nothing to be ashamed of.

She congratulated herself for having the foresight to have one of her teeth pulled a week earlier. The dentist wanted to save the tooth, but that procedure would have cost Mary Ann more than a week's salary. Her mouth felt fine now, and since the painful tooth had been far back in her mouth, no gap would be visible when she smiled.

Looking pert and radiant in her navy blue suit and yellow blouse, Mary Ann noticed that throughout their dinner, Paul Reynolds seemed to be staring at her in an approving manner.

Mary Ann believed that she was still thin enough to attract men. Though admittedly not as tall as she'd like to be, Mary Ann knew that her long, dark, curly hair seemed to add a few inches to her five-foot-two-inch frame.

Almost all the men she had ever dated had complimented her on her cute face. The high cheekbones prompted her ex-husband to nickname her "Cherokee."

Mary Ann was hoping that Paul would be unlike the last two men in her life, who showed only a short-lived interest in her. Both of these "prospects" had, no doubt, been chased away by the relationship restrictions of raising four young girls.

Paul, at five-foot-eleven-inches, was the tallest man she'd ever dated. He managed a local bank branch, was a widower ten years older than Mary Ann, and had no children.

Mary Ann had never before dined at a fancy French restaurant, and she had never tasted champagne. She decided afterwards that she liked both.

She couldn't help, though, equating the high prices on the restaurant's menu with the hard goods from her household budget. The cost of their dinner entrées would have gone a long way toward the purchase of two more beds for the girls. Mary Ann, too, was tired of sleeping every night on the cloth strips of a folding beach chair.

Eating on real china and using heavy silverware was also a treat. The plastic-like plates at home had only one virtue—they were unbreakable.

Mary Ann's attraction to Paul was increasing, and she enjoyed being alone with him during dinner. He seemed genuinely interested in her daily routine and life with the girls. Speaking about them so much made something inside of her miss their company.

Mary Ann remembered her last family dinner—at a restaurant outside Philadelphia. She had taken the girls to a Japanese steak house almost a year ago, courtesy of a radio station contest she had won. The girls all laughed when the Japanese cook, in the midst of his knife-flipping performance, took an egg out of his pocket and rolled it on the table.

"Japanese egg roll," the cook smiled.

At the end of Mary Ann's first evening with Paul, as she kissed him good night on the steps of her apartment, she became certain of at least one aspect of this advancing relationship.

Thinking about Paul's easy smile, wavy hair and sparkling blue eyes, Mary Ann admitted to herself that she was falling hard for this new man in her life. His kiss sparked a part of her she thought she had long since buried.

"I may not be in love yet," she analyzed, "but I'm definitely in lust."

෪

The light, pinkish sunburn covering her cheeks created a strong measure of radiance on Melissa's face. Even the most expensive of makeup preparations could never produce an equivalent glow.

Fluffy bangs, dangling earrings, and a touch of lipstick all added to her breezy, somewhat racy look.

She was also hoping to exude an air of confidence spiced with a pinch of youthful bearing—neither of which could be derived from cosmetics.

Melissa's attire began with a mostly white, black-patterned blouse having three-quarter-length sleeves. She wore a white, knee-length pleated skirt, black belt, and black heels. On her arm, she carried a white, knitted cardigan for later in the evening, when cooler air always wafted through and over the Florida Keys.

Melissa knew that a near constant smile was usually the best accessory for a well-dressed woman. And her anticipation that "Joe The Cop" might turn into a living, breathing, leading-man type was making it so much easier for her to manifest that smile. Helpful, too, was the fast-growing distance in hours since last night's tragic, disturbing accident.

When Melissa greeted Joe at the door of her room, she noticed right away that he was impressively dressed.

He wore a tan linen sport coat with a tiny monogram on the breast pocket. His summery brown slacks, cordovan loafers, and open-necked yellow sport shirt all seemed to complement his sparkling white teeth and curly hair. His deep, typically Florida tan acted as a counterpoint to her freshly sunburned cheeks.

Within minutes of his arrival, they were on their way to the Dolphin Harbor Inn—on the eastern end of Islamorada. En route, with him driving, Joe provided Melissa with additional good news, broadening her already bubbling smile.

"A truck belonging to one of the dead guys was found a few miles from here, in the parking lot of Ben and Dave's Marina," Joe informed. "We assume they were going to load this truck with the marijuana they had on board the boat.

"So, as of right now, there isn't even the slightest of lingering doubts about any illegal involvement on your part.

"The Monroe County detective told me that he hopes you enjoy the rest of your vacation here in Islamorada."

Melissa reveled in the news. And when Joe had finished his explanation, she brazenly stretched her body across the front seat of the car and kissed him, lightly, on the cheek.

"Calculated spontaneity," she told herself. "I can get away with this one. Even though he knows the reason behind it, he still might think that the kiss was at least partially motivated by how attractive I found him."

Melissa was truly relieved that all previous suspicions of her involvement had vanished as quickly as yesterday's weather forecasts. The situation was setting up as one with unfettered potential. A promising romantic involvement was now in view on her horizon.

She was hoping, perhaps optimistically, that her damsel-in-distress story, and Joe's rescue of her from the flaming pier, would be remembered solely for its novelty as a "how this couple met" story.

"And how did you two meet?" Melissa fantasized being asked—by someone, someday.

"Oh, nothing much out of the ordinary," Melissa would answer, tongue-in-cheek. "Joe just drove up in his police boat and plucked me from the throes of an inferno."

When they arrived for dinner, Melissa noticed that the Dolphin Harbor Inn had been built like a lean-to, jutting outward from an ancient-looking, restored lighthouse that had the distinction of being one of the first structures ever built in Islamorada. It dated back to 1909, when automobiles were novelties and wagons loaded with the catch of the day rattled along the dirt roads of what was then a sparsely populated fishing village.

Ocean-traveling ships would use the lighthouse's lone revolving beacon as a warning against the treacherous offshore reef.

Since Melissa and Joe arrived a few minutes ahead of their reservation, they took some time to stroll along the boat dock area that adjoined the lighthouse and restaurant.

"There are fifty boat slips at this dock," Joe told her. "Most of the boats are for sport fishing. They're all about thirty feet long and are for hire on a daily rate basis. The captains will take the fishermen out toward the offshore reef and try to catch marlin, sailfish, and even sharks."

"There are two large chairs with seat belts in that boat, over there," Melissa pointed. "What are they for?"

"Big fish require big chairs. If a fisherman hooks a monster of the deep, he doesn't want the fish to pull him into the water. Therefore, the seat belts."

Before Melissa could ask the next logical question—How big did the fish get?—she almost tripped over one of the largest sea creatures she had ever seen.

Sprawled out on the dock was a freshly caught marlin that looked to be about nine feet long. No doubt it could provide about five years' worth of canned food for her white cat, Coke, who was temporarily housed in a Philadelphia boarding kennel.

Also nearby, hanging on hooks, were several other large specimens— sailfish—that had been brought in earlier that day on the charter boats.

"What will the fishermen do with what they've caught?" Melissa inquired.

"The biggest of the fish will be stuffed and mounted by taxidermists. They'll end up as trophies in dens and living rooms from coast to coast, and even in some foreign countries. Islamorada attracts sport fishermen from all over the world."

"I saw a sign that listed the charter rates. Do fishermen really pay over four hundred dollars a day to go out on these boats?"

"During the height of the season, the price goes up. And the tourists can be seen every morning near dawn, holding their fishing gear while waiting in line for the privilege."

"I don't think I'd enjoy taking a ride on one of these boats. My stepfather let me tag along when I was a little girl. We went deep-sea fishing in Atlantic City and Ocean City. I remember a big, heavy boat, crowded with men, and the smell of bait. I also remember getting seasick on the way back—while I was watching the gulls circling overhead."

Once Melissa and Joe were seated at their table inside the restaurant, they were treated to a spectacular view of the now-radiant sunset and of the historical old lighthouse.

"There was a hurricane that wiped out this island back in 1935," Joe began. "The only locals who survived, except for a few who had gone to Miami to see the ball game, were six young highway workers who ran inside the lighthouse and climbed up to the top to wait out the storm. That painted line over there on the side of the lighthouse—at the eight-foot level—that's how high the water got during the worst part of the hurricane.

"It struck on the Sunday before Labor Day that year. Some of the waves were estimated at twenty feet high. A rescue train was sent in from Miami by the federal government. But the hurricane washed the train right off the tracks as soon as it got here. The locomotive, which weighed over a hundred tons, was the only thing left standing.

"The highway workers who were staying in town were building our current road, Route 1. The Miami to Key West section, right through the Keys, was constructed by itinerant laborers from the Works Progress Administration, the so-called W.P.A. There was no other highway. Aside from boats, the only way to get from one island to another back then was by railroad. But the train tracks, along with most of the towns along the way, were wiped out by the hurricane. The railroad was never rebuilt."

"That hurricane seemed terribly potent," Melissa commented. "Do they usually cause so much damage?" Melissa saw a faraway, almost pained look cross Joe's face for a brief moment before he continued on.

"The experts say the disastrous flooding was a result of the way Henry Flagler built that railroad of his. The high embankment next to the tracks prevented the water from washing its way through the island. Instead, the embankment acted like a dam, keeping the water level extremely high.

"One old timer, who lived in nearby Marathon, the next town between here and Key West, told me that the barometer went under twenty-seven during the hurricane. That's supposed to be some kind of meteorological record. Almost all of the Keys were devastated. The postmaster up in Key Largo had a total of forty-nine relatives living on the Keys before the storm, and only ten were still alive the day after the hurricane.

"Every once in a while, a skeleton turns up on one of the mangrove islands. And every couple of years, another old car is found half-buried somewhere—bearing 1935 license plates.

"After the storm, when Islamorada was rebuilt, the town council erected a monument to the dead highway workers. That monument is in the middle of a small park on the other side of the Seascaper, at Milepost 80."

"These highway workers, the W.P.A. people," Melissa inquired, "where did they come from? Were they from other parts of Florida, were they prisoners, or what?"

"Most of the laborers got the jobs because they were veterans of World War I. They were unemployed—victims of the Depression. And they moved from one tent city to another, following the highway. The famous author, Ernest Hemingway, who lived for a few years in Key West, wrote a magazine article soon after the storm. In it, he blamed the W.P.A. for not providing the workers with adequate shelter. He also criticized the lack of a prompt rescue.

"The only good thing that came out of the storm was the fact that the railroad bridges, which connected the long string of islands, were still standing. Even though the rail beds on land had been ripped apart, all of the railroad bridges from Miami straight through to Key West were in perfect shape.

"And since the W.P.A. had commissioned only the land portion of the overseas highway and had not yet gotten money to build the highway bridges, when they learned that the railroad would never be rebuilt, they turned the old railroad structures into highway bridges. This saved a lot of money as well as time. So, because of the hurricane and the destruction of the railroad, the overseas highway to Key West was finished several years ahead of schedule."

Melissa was fascinated by Joe's tale of Islamorada's history, and she told him so.

"You remind me of a very sexy history teacher I once had in college. Listening to him talk was a soothing experience—like when my stepfather used to tell me bedtime stories back when I still believed in the Easter Bunny.

"With all your attention to detail, you'd probably make a good librarian, too," Melissa added. "Did you ever consider going back to school to get a degree?"

"I have, but the 'Joe College' idea hasn't ever gotten past the thinking stage. It would be very difficult for me, what with my swing shift. One week I work days, the next week nights, and the third week my hours are midnight until eight o'clock in the morning."

After they had made several trips to the buffet table, which featured shrimp, king crab legs, scallops, and even barbecued ribs, Melissa decided that it was her turn to take hold of the imaginary microphone.

"I majored in history at Neuva Villa, a small women's college near Pittsburgh. I have pleasant memories of my years in the dorm with all the friends I made. I loved the all-night study sessions, the weekend parties on campus, and the long train rides home for the holidays. Sometimes, I wish I could go back in time and be a college sophomore again.

"After finishing college, I went straight into graduate work, taking library science. When I got my master's, I was lucky to find a job right away in a reference department.

"I can't stand library cataloguing, which is highly computerized now. And I didn't want to be a children's librarian. I just wouldn't have the patience to work with kids. Reference was the only thing I ever wanted to do.

"When I see professional librarians entertaining kiddies by reading to them aloud during so-called story hours, I feel sick to my stomach. I'm kind of funny when it comes to children's literature, or 'kiddy lit.' Aside from a handful of classics, most of it is junk. I'm positive that any bright college student with a flair for storytelling could out-write most of the people who pass themselves off as children's authors.

"So, I guess I've been extremely happy as a reference librarian. I have no career complaints. It's challenging work with both the general public and with the university types—answering their questions and directing them to the most useful research sources. I was a great help to my ex-husband, who taught poetry and advanced composition. I hope he learned something from my help, so that he can do his scholarly papers by himself now.

"My job has its humorous moments, too, like when I get phone calls from people who want answers to trivia questions. I got a real challenge last summer when the same woman called me two weeks in a row—both times on Monday mornings. Her first question was 'How many dimples are there on a golf ball?' and her next question was 'How many seeds are there in a watermelon?' It took me a while, but I found both of the answers for her. One can only wonder, though, what she intended to do with the information."

"Did you pick up a golf ball," Joe asked, "and count the dimples yourself?"

"No, that's not kosher," Melissa explained. "A reference librarian's job is to find a written source that gives the correct information."

"Golf balls and watermelons! There are books, you say, that can tell us how many seeds are in a watermelon! How ridiculous!" Joe exclaimed. "I just can't help but think how your job is such a petty pursuit compared to police work. We're saving lives and arresting crooks, while you're answering trivia questions."

"I guess reference work is just about as stupid," Melissa cracked, with a smile, "as cops who write out jaywalking tickets or put grandmothers in jail for playing bingo."

"Touché, touché."

The key lime pie that Melissa and Joe ate for dessert was delicious. Melissa even went back to the trifle tray for a second helping. And at just about the time she had finished consuming the last scrumptious bite, Joe started telling her about his workaday life as one of Islamorada's finest.

"There are just four of us in the department, full-time. We have a grand total of three patrol cars and two boats. The job is comfortable for me in that it's not boring, probably much the same as what you'd see on a realistic television show. Since this is a tourist town, I get to meet unusual people once in awhile. And, occasionally, as with the boat accident, there's a bit of an intellectual challenge.

"I don't think I could be a policeman in a big city, though. There would seem to be too many dangerous midnight calls when my life would be on the line. And although the people down here in Islamorada are not all saintly, at least they're sane. If I had to deal with the crazies you find in a metropolitan area like Miami, well, they couldn't pay me enough money.

"I was born and raised in Baltimore. After my parents died in a car accident when I was twelve, I went to live with my uncle in New Jersey. Then I joined the Marines right after high school.

"I spent two years as the captain's steward on a Navy cruiser. I was just a glorified butler, but it was easy duty.

"We sailed along in the Mediterranean most of the time, practicing how to stay afloat, I guess. My last two years were at the Marine base in Quantico, Virginia. When I was there, ironically, they put me in charge of training new recruits in jungle warfare. I instructed the grunts in what to expect if our country ever goes to war again.

"So there I was," Joe laughed, "a Marine sergeant who'd never even been close to a battle trying to train rookies in how to survive the front lines!

"After I was discharged, I stayed in Miami with John Olivera, one of my Marine buddies. I learned to love Florida's year-round warm weather—and the swimming. The fishing was great, too, except for the time I went spear fishing. I found out the hard way that when you hit a fish with a spear, the spilled blood draws sharks. One of the biggest frights I ever had was scurrying back onto the deck of a boat within spitting distance of this huge shark fin.

"John and I had a lot of good times together in Miami. Being young, unattached, and suddenly free from the Marine discipline, we would, on more than one occasion, drink to our health until we collapsed.

"I was entitled to veteran's preference bonus points when Monroe County gave its patrolman's exam. I passed the test with a high mark, and I've been here ever since."

At the conclusion of their dinner, Joe suggested a drive to the Sleepy Turtle Restaurant, which was just a short hop down the road.

"We'll have a nightcap. You'll just love the décor," he promised.

Before they could even walk through the front door, Melissa saw what Joe was referring to. Decked out on the roof of the building were six-foot-high papier-mâché statues of turtles, comprising a turtle family. The likenesses were, of course, dressed for the holiday season, with red trim accentuating their natural green bodies.

There was a Santa Claus turtle, a Mrs. Claus turtle, and kid turtles— all smiling and standing around a brightly decorated, authentic Christmas tree. Even the treetop ornament was a turtle.

Inside the restaurant were pictures of turtles, plush turtle dolls hanging from the rafters, and more turtle statues. The featured dish on the dinner menu was, of course, turtle chowder.

Melissa and Joe spent almost two hours at the Sleepy Turtle, talking about everything from his fascination with the watching of major league baseball games to her own favorite pastimes—crossword puzzles and mystery novels.

Melissa also discovered that Joe liked to attend horse races, dog races, and pro-football games.

Melissa told him he might enjoy meeting her stepfather, who was also a horseracing fan.

When their evening together had finally ended, and Joe had dropped her off at the Seascaper, he suggested that they spend a few hours the next day exploring the local beaches.

"We can look for conch shells, do a little swimming, and I'll even show you the hurricane monument," he added. Melissa again noticed that same pained look cross Joe's face, and she couldn't help but wonder what deep hurt lay buried behind Joe's friendly eyes.

However, at this point in their budding relationship, Melissa would have agreed to a tour of bombed-out buildings, greasy spoon diners, or even the lobby of a rural post office—such was her attraction to a cop named Joe.

They kissed each other good night, ever so briefly, yet tenderly, at the door of her room. Joe's kiss was all that Melissa had dreamed it would be—strong and definitely compassionate. It was, she hoped, a harbinger of the good things yet to come.

Melissa waved to him as he drove off, once again feeling a rush of impending romance—the kind that turns teenagers into one-track fantasy machines and women of all ages into carefree dreamers.

Then, alone in her room, she wished that her white alley cat, Coke, could be with her.

It was at times like these, when the good things happened, that she liked to report to Coke. Vocally, she'd describe everything positive that she had just experienced—whether it was to tell a tale about a funny incident at the library or to talk without being interrupted about a book she had just finished reading or a play she had recently attended.

For Melissa, Coke served as a diary without pages or a tape recorder that could never be played back. And, regardless of what Melissa would tell her, Coke would remain mute, never criticizing.

"It's a good thing your name isn't Grass," Melissa laughed, pretending that Coke was purring at her feet. "If it were, Joe might have second thoughts when he meets you."

Chapter 4

The coffee and cola would have to keep her awake. It was 6 a.m., and Mary Ann had just finished working the all-night shift at her weekend cashier's job. She normally tried to catch an hour or two of rest before reporting to work, but she was unable to do so this time. Melissa had another asthma attack that frightened her and kept her from going to bed on time. "Oh well," thought Mary Ann, "that's what being a mother is all about."

She punched out, left the convenience store with a bottle of soda, and walked home.

Within an hour, Paul had arrived, ready for their trip to the horse stables. Paul was the owner of two racehorses in a partnership with one of his co-workers.

Mary Ann had never visited a racetrack stable area. Melissa, her only daughter not allergic to horsehair, would accompany them. As a precaution, though, Mary Ann brought along the pulmonary-inhaling machine that her girls used for asthma emergencies.

Owning a horse of her own was one of Mary Ann's long-time fantasies. The farm next to her parents' boarded horses, and she often spent many an afternoon as a child wondering what it would be like to ride one of those beautiful creatures. She would often daydream about riding her horse, alone, along a snow-covered path in the mountains—far removed from buildings, highways, and people. In reality, the closest she'd ever come to actually owning a horse was her collection of coffee mugs—20 all told—each decorated with the colorful likeness of a horse—some in action scenes and others standing motionless in their own majesty.

Mary Ann and Melissa petted Paul's horses, fed them carrots, and took turns walking them around the barn. Melissa made friends with a huge gray cat, who purred constantly while rubbing his body against her sneakers and floppy white sox.

The trainer who worked for Paul offered coffee and doughnuts, and because of the cool morning breezes, Mary Ann was glad she'd chosen to wear the fur jacket Paul had recently given her.

Paul was impressed with how Mary Ann got along so well with all of the horses in the racetrack barn. She showed no fear, walking up to each of thirty or so stalls and stroking every one as if it had been a family pet for many years.

"In high school, I was always a wallflower," she told Paul. "All I had was my seashell collection and my daydreams. Now I've blossomed, off-the-wall. If nobody was looking, I'd lead one of these beautiful animals home and keep him in my backyard."

Afterwards, Paul took Mary Ann and Melissa out for lunch—at a seafood restaurant that specialized in shrimp omelets and homemade, high-calorie desserts.

Then, as they neared home, the trio made one final stop—at Mary Ann's urging.

"I want you to see this little coffee shop I just love," Mary Ann told Paul. "It's where I bought some of my horse mugs. They also have a counter where we can sit and relax for a while."

French Brandy Espresso was the flavor of the day at Coffee, Tea & Ye, and Mary Ann paid for two cups, plus Melissa's soda. It made her feel good to treat Paul for a change and share with him a place that was one of her favorites.

"I walk over here a couple of times every month," Mary Ann explained. "I like to try the different coffee flavors. It's also a cheap night out.

"With all the expensive, fattening food and the gifts you've been giving me lately, I might start to put on some extra poundage—mentally and physically—that I probably shouldn't.

"I hope," she smiled, "that you aren't going to spoil me."

❦

Joe met Melissa early the next morning. Their first bit of business was to enjoy a leisurely breakfast together at the Seascaper. Afterwards, they headed for the first stop on Joe's informal tour—the hurricane monument.

There wasn't a whole lot to see, really. The monument was more like a micro-mini version of a war memorial in a town square.

Located in a tiny, half-acre park site just off Route 1 (everything in Islamorada is just off Route 1), the hurricane monument was a gravestone-like tablet, about five feet square, perched at the top of a wide, ten-step marble stairway.

Engraved on the austere face of it was a bleak scene showing clumps of shadowy palm trees, wet and bent wildly from the wind. These images framed the names of about two hundred persons known to have died in the hurricane of 1935.

As with all monuments, gravestones, and the like, Melissa was compelled to feel it—to rub her hand across the names that had been cut into the stone—as if her fingers could communicate with the silent souls of the drowned.

"The names, out here in the sun forever, are a nice touch," Melissa commented. "The beautiful weather here in the Florida Keys could shine on this monument for eternity. The first and last names of the dead will benefit from thousands, maybe millions of days of warm air and cool, soothing breezes. If you want to be remembered after you die, you can't ask for a better, more impressive setting."

"You're absolutely right," Joe concurred, as they started to walk back to his car. "Their bodies may have disappeared into nothingness, but the monument connects each of them with the lives they lived on this island. It also gives them sort of a team identity—as if they were the Class of 1935.

"Now and then, though, I think about what my responsibilities would be some day, as a policeman, if another big hurricane were to hit Islamorada. Our police emergency plan stresses evacuation only—in other words, get in the car and head straight for Miami, as fast as you can.

"There really are no adequate shelters here, no mountains to climb to avoid the high water. And as for tall buildings, they just don't exist."

"Do you think everyone here would be able to get away, safely, from another hurricane?"

"I'm not sure," Joes continued, pensively. "It's true that we have a better communication system these days, compared with 1935, what with so much television and radio. So, everyone ought to know well in advance that a hurricane is due to strike. The federal government, though, would probably have to help us out by sending in some fast boats and helicopters."

"What do you mean?"

"There are just too many people living on the Keys now, Melissa. With the permanent population gradually creeping upward and the trend today toward year-round Florida tourism, you might be talking about putting tens of thousands of people on only one highway, at the same time, going in one direction.

"From Key West all the way back to Miami, where they could get some decent shelter, is about a hundred and fifty miles. So if Key West were the site of a hurricane's probable landfall, that could mean a hundred and fifty miles of bumper-to-bumper traffic."

"As a policeman, then, you wouldn't be allowed to jump in your car and go along with the crowd, would you?"

"No, I'd be obligated to stay. First, I'd have to knock on doors to make sure that everyone knew about the storm. Next, I'd have to arrange some sort of cooperative transportation for those people who had no way out—car pools, maybe. And, finally, I'd have to wait until the last of the traffic had passed through. There are some eighty miles of highway from Key West to where we're standing in Islamorada. And no doubt some of those frightened, scurrying tourists would have car trouble somewhere in this town.

"I'm afraid, Melissa, that I'd be one of the last to get out."

"Charming thought," Melissa added, wryly, in commiseration with Joe's dismal projection. "Obviously, a monster hurricane would be God's way to even the score after blessing this place with so many days of warm, delicious weather."

As she spoke, Melissa wondered, silently, about the level of Joe's concern over hurricanes. Was it something he dreaded constantly, or just occasionally? Or did he consider it only a remote possibility that really didn't affect him at all? While she pondered, he answered.

"I'm probably foolish, but I'm probably also like most of the other people who live here. We very rarely think about it, we never talk about it, and deep down inside we have this cocksure confidence that we're quicker and craftier than any hurricane nature can muster. A little bit of wind and rain, that's all they are."

This answer didn't quite dispel Melissa's suspicions that something else lurked behind Joe's statement. It was almost like he was trying to convince himself of his ability to overcome a hurricane. That wince of pain that flickered through his eyes as he spoke about hurricanes seemed to speak to a deep sorrow. Melissa suspected she was about to tread on dangerous ground, but this was the "new" Melissa, and if she was to have an open relationship she was determined that there'd be no secrets.

"Joe, I can't help but notice that the mention of hurricanes brings some real pain to your eyes. Is there something you're not telling me?" Melissa grabbed Joe's hand instinctively, but let her eyes drop to the ground, afraid to watch Joe's reaction to this question.

Joe shuddered slightly, then pulled Melissa down to sit on a nearby bench. He looked out to sea for a few minutes before he spoke again. "It's been a while since I have talked about this to anyone, but many years ago, back when I was based at Quantico, I was engaged to a nurse who lived in Cherry Hill, New Jersey, not far from my uncle in Somerdale.

"We had met one summer at a local bar there while I was visiting my uncle, and we just clicked. Before I knew it, we were engaged. We were planning to get married right after my tour of duty was over. Becky was a pediatric nurse, and really dedicated to her patients at Children's Hospital in Philadelphia. She just didn't want to leave the area. So we put off the wedding until we could find housing together somewhere near her job.

"Then Hurricane Agnes came. It wasn't that horrible a storm as hurricanes go, especially in the Northeast. But Becky was traveling to work during the worst part of the storm. The roads were pretty washed out from all the rain and visibility was pretty poor. She was only two miles from the bridge to Philadelphia when a tractor-trailer skidded and lost control, plowing right into her. The police said she never knew what hit her. She died instantly.

"I've never really felt the same for anyone since."

Joe finally turned to look at Melissa, and she saw his eyes filled with tears. She squeezed his hand, and rested her head on his shoulder unable to say anything that seemed appropriate after such a tale.

They sat for a few more moments, and then Joe stood up, pulled Melissa to her feet, and said, "Let's move on, shall we?" Melissa smiled in relief that the sparkle was back in Joe's eyes again.

Thus, with worries over hurricane sanity finally put to bed, the next stop on the duo's itinerary was the beach at nearby Caloosa Cove.

At the far southwestern point of Islamorada, just before the bridge that marked the end of Joe's official police jurisdiction, was a secluded beach hidden off the ocean side of the highway. To get to it, Joe drove his car down a slight, unpaved incline and over some very bumpy terrain.

"It looks like sand we're riding on," Melissa offered, as she bounced slightly on her seat and literally had to hold onto her sunhat with one hand, "but it's not very soft."

"Just a few more yards," Joe laughed. "This is a far cry from the beaches in New Jersey. The islands in South Florida were formed from hard coral. There's no soft sand."

When Joe stopped the car, close to the water's edge, Melissa was captivated immediately by the picturesque view. Spread out before them was a dictionary definition of the word "magnificent." A wide expanse of pure white beach was accented by calm, minute ripples of seawater that sparkled before them, from right to left as far as the eye could see and straight out to the cloudless horizon.

The beach was deserted except for the tiny, sandpiper-like birds who didn't fly much but who hustled along on feet moving so fast that only a blur was visible. There were hundreds of these birds, and they seemed to change directions in groups, as if they were miniature soldiers practicing their marches on a military parade ground.

Huge palm trees provided occasional shade from the eighty-five degree sunshine. The trees, most of which bore clusters of greenish coconuts poised far above ground level, no doubt began their lives by bursting through the shallow dirt before snaking skyward like so many crooked secondary roadways.

Sprinkled haphazardly throughout the beach were wild, purplish-hued hibiscus bushes that helped paint a truly tropical scene.

Surprisingly, there were no waves at all breaking in the surf.

"The approaching swells slice through the coral reef long before reaching the shoreline," Joe noted. "The offshore water is always calm here, as if it were one big, gigantic swimming pool."

Melissa was the first one to leave the car. As part of a magnetic reaction to the closeness of the sea, she slipped out of her tee shirt and slacks, revealing a red-and-blue, flowered bikini that was a shade more conservative than racy.

"Let's try the water," she beamed, holding her hands to her hips and waiting as Joe started a mild struggle to kick off his trousers.

From the way Joe kept shifting his gaze from Melissa to his clothes and back again, she was sure that her suddenly undraped, thin, shapely figure was definitely to his liking.

Joe's strong, athletic build was also a turn-on. Melissa liked his rippling, muscular body and the way a clump of grayish-black hairs contrasted with his deep, dark tan. This salt-and-pepper hair pattern seemed to be in coordination, naturally, with his white-and-black striped trunks.

Melissa started to trot, gingerly, toward the water's edge, but she stopped abruptly after the bottoms of her feet encountered hundreds of tiny, painful shells.

As if on cue, Joe reached out to hold her hand.

"Whatever you do, don't walk on the blue things that look like broken balloons," he advised. "They're a form of jellyfish that can give you a nasty sting."

"There are shells everywhere," Melissa exclaimed, pointing toward the ground. "And they're so small."

She reached down to pick up a handful of crushed coral, filled with shells, and marveled further at what she observed.

"Look, Joe, I must have at least a dozen of them in my hand. They're all different colors, and some are smaller than contact lenses. But I can tell that all of them are definitely conch shells. Miniature conch shells. I've collected a few of the bigger ones at beaches up north, usually right after a storm has hit, but I've never seen any this small. The ones I have at home are about the size of baseballs."

"Later on we'll make it a point to collect some of the nicer ones—to add to your collection," Joe smiled, as he led the way into the water. "We'll get big shells, small shells, and shells that you'll need a microscope to enjoy. The really big ones found here in the Keys—those that measure maybe twelve inches across—are used for horns. A skilled native of the 'Conch Republic'—as Key Westers like to call themselves—can blow into a dried conch shell and make a sound like a tugboat horn. And it doesn't require strong lung power, just the ability to hold your lips a certain way when blowing through the shell.

"By the way, have you ever eaten any conch?"

"Yes, I have. The last time I visited the Keys I had some. And I remember that conch chowder tastes great, much better than clam chowder."

While they stood at wading level, gleefully splashing each other for several minutes, Joe told Melissa the story of the horse conchs and the queen conchs.

"Not too many northerners know the difference between the two types of conchs. The shells look the same, but the queens are vegetarians, eating algae and the greens that grow on the ocean floor. The horse conchs, however, are carnivorous. And the one thing the horse conchs feed on, believe it or not, are the queen conchs. They sneak behind the queen conchs like this," Joe whispered, as he deftly swooped up Melissa, with ease, into his strong arms, "and then they wait for them to come out of their shells before they gobble 'em up."

With that, he ran backwards for a few steps farther into the surf, gently releasing Melissa's body. Then he fell into a backstroke in the deeper water.

When Melissa came up for air, her hair now straight and her face completely soaked, she was laughing hysterically.

"My oldest sister was the last one who did that to me," she screamed, the warm sun reflecting its light off her cheeks, "and that was when I was six years old."

In all, Melissa and Joe spent about twenty more minutes in the water—swimming, wading, and playfully splashing about. Then they returned, wet and exhausted, to the blanket they had spread on the beach, near Joe's car. While they sat, looking out at the surf and drying off quickly in the now much warmer sun, Joe pointed in the distance to a small spot of coastline off to the left, about a mile down the beach.

"When the sun's right, you can see my trailer from here."

"What trailer?"

"Aha, that's a typical city dweller. My trailer is where I live."

"You mean you live in a mobile home?"

"It may be possible to make it a mobile home again, but I've never moved it. There are so many palm trees and hibiscus bushes growing alongside and through the outside walls that it's probably rooted in the coral by now. It might even be hurricane proof."

"I've noticed quite a few mobile homes between here and the southern side of Miami, especially around Key Largo. But I don't recall ever being inside one. What are they like?"

"Mine is crowded with furniture, to be honest, but kind of cozy. It's a nice place for me. Doesn't take much effort to clean. It's a little bigger than most trailers, called a 'double-wide.' I have a small bedroom, an even tinier living room, and, despite what you city slickers might think, indoor plumbing. I also have a sign in one of the windows that says 'Beware of Dog,' but there's no dog. I live alone, just Joe Carlton, no girlfriend, no wife.

"So, tell me, what kind of a place do you have in Philadelphia?"

"I own a large-sized twin. It's a corner property in a city neighborhood. I've been living there for almost six years now, and I've grown accustomed to the place. When Brady left, I thought the house would be like a museum, with empty spaces that I'd never use. It didn't turn out that way, though. His old den is filled up with houseplants now. And I've turned the spare bedroom into my own private library.

"So, instead of piling up my old paperback books into some corner and then throwing them out after they've attracted a few layers of dust, I now have a place to keep them. I don't have to feel guilty any more about tossing a book into a trashcan.

"Thanks to Brady, there's no longer a mortgage to pay, and the taxes are cheap. It's only a ten-minute drive to my library. I have some friends who live near me and others who live in the center of town. And the block I live on has quite a few families. Even though I, personally, have never entertained any thoughts about raising kids of my own, the families, I must admit, give it a certain stability that I find more comfortable than Philly's downtown area.

"I'm still attracted to the cultural events in the center of town, the shows, the restaurants, and just the overall ambiance. Usually, once or twice a week, I'll travel the thirty minutes to center city Philadelphia to meet a friend for an evening's entertainment."

The now blazing Islamorada sun, which was no doubt pushing the temperature near the ninety degree mark, provided for a quick drying-off period. Within minutes, sporting dry bathing suits, Melissa and Joe began to walk, hand-in-hand, near the water's edge.

Joe had fetched a small plastic bag from the trunk of his car, and Melissa was using it to hold the most beautiful of tiny conch shells that she was picking up—at an almost constant pace.

During their half-hour walk along the beach, Melissa and Joe spent as much time gazing into each other's eyes as they did looking at the scenery. After collecting maybe a hundred different conch shells, they started their drive back toward the center of Islamorada.

They stopped for a snack along the way at a roadside luncheonette that featured Cuban cuisine. The menu in the restaurant window, aside from listing various delicacies spelled out in Spanish, also proclaimed "Regular Meals, Regular Dinners," which, Melissa discovered, meant hot dogs and hamburgers.

The morning exercise had given them strong appetites. Eating quickly, they seemed to inhale their burgers and fries. Joe topped off the meal with a Cuban-style fried banana. Melissa declined.

"Whatever you do during your stay in the Keys," Joe advised, "don't give in to any urges to buy coconuts or key limes. If you want to take some freshly grown samples home with you, I know exactly where to look for free food. I can guide you to the best-tasting, wildest-growing coconuts, key limes, and even grapefruit—which, by the way, is still in season."

Joe then drove Melissa to another small beach called Witch's Point, on the north side of the island. After stripping to their bathing suits again and wading out to waist level, they stopped, looked into each other's eyes, ever so briefly, and then reached out, simultaneously, to embrace one another. Their glistening, warmly wet bodies remained fused together for several minutes while their lips consummated an impassioned kiss.

When they finally broke, they began pecking again almost immediately, lip to lip, before returning again to a deep, full-fledged, wraparound kiss.

Melissa felt only minor excitement initially, except for the comforting strength of Joe's arms and the quivering motion of the muscles in his lips. Further into the second kiss, however, when his tongue massaged hers, Melissa's mind was triggered into fantasy, drifting off into short, rocket blasts of thought scattered among remembrances of the popping of champagne corks, autumn leaves at their golden finest, and sunrise on a clear mountain lake.

When they released each other, turned, and headed back toward Joe's car, Melissa flooded her brain waves with a strong wish that this idyllic day, so full of promise, would never end—as if it were the ultimate twenty-four hour period that could never be equaled, and anything that dared to come afterward would be doomed as anticlimactic.

On the drive back to Melissa's room, Joe apologized for having to return so quickly to his police work. He was scheduled to start a double shift later that evening.

"I'd love to spend the rest of the day—and the night—with you," he admitted. "But I really must work sixteen straight hours beginning at six o'clock tonight. Then I get a few hours off to sleep before working another shift—from tomorrow afternoon to tomorrow night. I'd like to make a suggestion, though, that I think you might like."

"Try me."

"Day after tomorrow we trek on down to Key West for two days. We'll do some sightseeing along the way, find a place to stay in the southernmost town in the continental United States, then toot around the historic sites the following day.

"Are you game?"

"That's the best offer I've had in years."

Chapter 5

Three deliverymen came to Mary Ann's door on Friday afternoon.

When she unwrapped the bouquet of roses and carnations, it was as if she'd turned on a light to illuminate the semi-darkness of her kitchen. Flowers that were brightly colored and aromatic had always fascinated Mary Ann. She loved to smell them, having pressed her nose to thousands of petals ever since childhood.

Just last year, she had planted petunias, snapdragons, and portulacas outside her apartment, next to the walkway, but a group of neighborhood boys had trampled on some of the young growths and had uprooted others.

The additional gifts from Paul that awaited Mary Ann included a bottle of Chanel No. 5 and a terry cloth bathrobe.

"A lady must always have a robe," Paul had recently told her, after she'd admitted to not owning one.

Paul and Mary Ann were planning a weekend tour of nearby Delaware, stopping at museums and perhaps spending an evening at the racetrack near Wilmington.

"My last out-of-town trip was back in October," Mary Ann told Paul. "I took the girls on a bus ride to New York City, and then we got on a boat to visit the Statue of Liberty.

"I'll never forget the look on Melissa's face after I gave her the money to pay for our lunch at that little restaurant in Manhattan. I was already out on the sidewalk with the rest of the girls, waiting for her, when she ran up to us and said, 'Mommy, the man at the cash register must have gotten me mixed up with somebody else. He didn't take my money, and he gave me $17. He said it was my change.'"

"You'll like what you see in Delaware," Paul advised. "After we stop at the Hagley Mansion and walk along the Brandywine Creek, we'll visit the gardens at Winterthur. I know you've called me a 'rich' person several times already, but this DuPont fellow who designed the gardens had so much money that he could afford to collect trees from around the world. He planted hundreds of different types throughout the grounds on his estate."

And although she found the landscaping at Winterthur to be indeed beautiful, Mary Ann fell in love instead with the magnolia tree that was in full bloom right outside the door of their motel room. She insisted that Paul take her picture as she stood amidst the purple-colored blossoms.

Inside that room, Mary Ann and Paul would make love for the first time, and Mary Ann was prepared—having packed her suitcase with two scented candles. "A special touch," she thought, for a special occasion.

"Peppermint. They're peppermint candles," she told a sniffing Paul, laughingly, as they lay on the bed—hard in each other's embrace.

Mary Ann giggled again when she told Paul that his large, uncircumcised penis looked like a fire hose. And he, surprised by her frank, childlike commentary, giggled in return. Since she had borne four children, Mary Ann was convinced that even an extra-large penis would not be painful to her.

While she and Paul began their breathtaking, inaugural act of love, Mary Ann's mind raced back to her early high school days. She and her girlfriend, Sherry, were still virgins when they first fantasized about orgasms. Her coupling now with Paul far exceeded those fantasies.

In their motel the following morning, Mary Ann woke up before Paul. First, she purposefully gazed throughout the room and then walked around busily, tossing the clothing from her suitcase and flipping the plastic pages of her wallet, trying to find something, anything that she could give to Paul at the moment he awoke. An old photograph of her perhaps, or any small, meaningful memento would only help to increase the strength of their growing bond.

She had a craving to please this gentle, thoughtful man to whom she felt she owed the life-tasting rebirth she was now experiencing.

Mary Ann left the room briefly, and when she returned, she sat on the bed alongside Paul's feet, watching his eyelids while she waited.

"Here, drink this," she smiled, as soon as he awoke. "It's a cold glass of water. And if you want a refill, there's more ice."

Despite being in Islamorada—a luxurious vacation setting—Melissa spent what she considered a boring day on Saturday. She had gotten used to Joe's company and accustomed to the way the hours seemed to fly by with him at her side. On this day, though, she found herself staring at her watch—and at various clocks—from dawn until evening. So, even in the face of continued warm weather, it was, figuratively, a day without sunshine.

Her constant thoughts during this contemplative, intervening period centered on the unknown activities that awaited her during the proposed forty-eight-hour visit to Key West—scheduled to begin tomorrow.

Melissa's daydreaming touched on all aspects of a possible serious relationship with Joe. Primarily, she fantasized about the ultimate— marriage—and whether she could ever consider living with him in Islamorada, or, in the alternative, if Joe would consent to relocating to Philadelphia. True, his uncle, his only remaining relative, lived in nearby New Jersey, but with so many painful memories of Becky linked there, could he handle such a move?

Also putting her psyche on edge was the distinct likelihood of sex in Key West. Did spending the night away from Islamorada mean they would be sharing a single motel room? Would Joe be expecting her to provide sex? Did he purposely give her a day without him so she could have time to convince herself that sex would be an acceptable complement to this overnight vacation within a vacation?

What does Joe hope to gain by taking her to Key West? Is his only motive a one-night stand? Does he flirt with every tourist the same way? A week from now, will he be charming some vacationer from Minnesota and taking her to the same local attractions?

There were questions, many questions. But also, there was hope.

☞

Early on Sunday morning, Joe stopped by the Seascaper to pick up Melissa. As she'd promised him, she was dressed casually. On the left portion of her white blouse was a wide, vertical red stripe that ran from the collar to the belt line. Her short, white linen skirt and white sneakers completed the outfit, giving her the look of a tennis player—or perhaps even a cheerleader.

After they had greeted each other, Melissa fixed her eyes on Joe's facial expression, looking for smirks that could be interpreted as signs of lust or anticipation of sexual conquest. She could, however, discern no hints of either. In fact, he was able to maintain his gentlemanly smile even after opening the trunk of the car and placing her overnight bag next to his.

"Joe's probably a very good poker player," Melissa thought, as she thanked him for holding open the car door. "Putting my bag away would have been the perfect time for a wisecrack."

Melissa briefly considered a flippant comment of her own, like, "Did you bring the prophylactics, Joe, or should I go back and get some?" She decided, however, to hold her tongue.

Melissa knew, though, that the day ahead would be a much more pleasurable experience if the air were cleared right away about the evening's sleeping arrangements.

So, almost as soon as the car had accelerated to fifty-five miles per hour on Route 1, Melissa uttered the inevitable question. She offered it in an indirect, casual fashion, letting Joe know that she was aware of the possibilities, but at the same time giving him an opportunity to ask her about her preference—or to provide an option.

"Did you make a reservation for one room or for two?"

"Actually, I made a pair of reservations," he answered. "The Jones reservation at one motel is for a single room. The Carlton/Tomlinson reservation at another motel is for two rooms. Sometime today, either now or later, you can tell me whether you'd be more comfortable as Mrs. Jones or as Miss Tomlinson."

"Did you bring the prophylactics?" Melissa asked him, giving an indirect but obvious answer. "Or should we stop along the way and buy a few?"

Joe grinned sheepishly and replied, "I think we're covered."

∞

The nearly two-hour drive to Key West took them across what seemed like endless stretches of water covered by hundreds of arching highway bridges, some of which were longer and larger than the islands they joined.

The twenty-odd "major" Keys that form the archipelago were dotted with sparsely populated, New England–type towns, most looking like board-by-board restorations of American fishing villages circa 1950. On Ramrod Key, possibly the most typical, a trailer park and a few tiny bungalows were clustered around a general store that bore a tired, wooden façade.

In each town along the way, almost to a shingle, the centrally located commercial building, which usually bore the sign of a major gasoline company, was bordered on the rear by a bayside dock—with the obligatory fuel pump for servicing local boaters.

Joe stopped the car only once on the way to Key West, about halfway from Islamorada. The spot he picked was on the edge of Marathon, just before the start of the so-called Seven Mile Bridge, the longest span linking the Keys.

Their parking spot off to the side of the highway was at the point where the bridge ramp left the land and began its skyward climb.

As they walked down toward the nearby shoreline, they could see miles of clear water, both blue and bluish-green, in every direction. Faintly visible, near the horizon, was a tiny section of the next nearest island, where this gracefully designed bridge, seemingly bound for infinity, would once again meet highway.

As Melissa's eyes tracked the westward path of this mammoth steel structure, she thought it similar to a star trail or the flight of a meteor that could splash down anywhere at all in this vast expanse of water but chose instead to settle on a remote sliver of land, far into the distance, that looked to be but a tiny toy in God's gigantic hot tub.

Joe, too, seemed awestruck.

"I love to stop here and gaze at the water," he confided, with one foot propped on a bulkhead. "I can do it for hours on end. If I ever need a little time by myself to think and to clear my mind, I seek out an ocean, and I just stare."

"I guess I get the same kind of a high you're describing when I look into my fireplace on cold and windy winter evenings," Melissa observed, "or when I travel to the New Jersey shore and sit on one of those board-walk benches, watching the whitecaps crashing onto the beach."

"Fire and water are powerful symbols."

"You're right, Joe. Maybe that's why I always come away with a silent confidence, as if I've just completed some sort of prayerful penance."

Hand-in-hand now, they walked back up the sandy incline and kissed, ever so briefly, before continuing their southwestward journey.

◈

Melissa's first impression of Key West was that it was a cross between Bourbon Street in New Orleans and Fisherman's Wharf in San Francisco.

Key West's steamy weather, the narrow streets, and the mix of black and white bodies in various stages of undress—bikinis, Bermuda shorts, and tee shirts galore—put it on a definite par with New Orleans' French Quarter.

A preponderance of sidewalk restaurants, large yachts berthed just off the main street, and oddly costumed street people were reminiscent of San Francisco's waterfront.

Joe told her that the best sightseeing plan would be to drive through the most interesting parts of town prior to any walking they might do later. And while they were cruising in the car, Melissa noticed just as many bicycles and mopeds vying for roadway space as there were auto-mobiles.

"Ernest Hemingway lived right over there," Joe pointed, "in that big house behind the red brick fence. He was a cat fancier, just like you. We can take a tour through the house during our stay, if you like. There are still about fifty cats that roam the grounds. Legend has it they're all descendants of the pets that Ernest once owned."

Farther on, in Mallory Square, at the center of the tourist area, Joe drove by the Key West Aquarium, where the featured attraction was a large, open swimming pool for sharks.

Close by the aquarium was the John James Audubon building, which contained an exhibit of colorful and finely detailed bird paintings—all done by America's foremost ornithologist. Melissa could tell at a glance, from the realism of the feathers, beaks, and eyes, that Audubon had dedicated thousands of hours to bird watching. She also knew that he painted from the carcasses of the birds he had killed.

The easy and informative way that Joe described the importance of the local sites was impressive to Melissa. The more he talked, the more intelligent he seemed. And although the true essence of Key West may be more honky-tonk than haute couture, Joe's descriptive commentaries—on the early Key West pirates, their jewelry, and their galleons—infused an aura of anecdotal history that rivaled the tales associated with Russia's Winter Palace, with England's Tower of London, or with Greece's Parthenon.

Likewise, his knowledgeable dissertation on Key West's homesteaders made him appear kin to dozens of scholarly Sunday afternoon lecturers that Melissa had chanced hearing on her casual visits to renowned museums in New York and Philadelphia.

Jutting out from the southernmost tip of the island was a long fishing pier, about five times the size of the Seascaper's. After Joe stopped the car at the entrance to the pier, he and Melissa began walking toward the far end, arm-in-arm—as if sheltering each other from the increasing strength of the wind. They were treading noisily over the wooden planks when he asked her if she were nervous.

"Not as long as you're with me," Melissa whispered, confidently, clutching Joe's shoulder just a little tighter as she spoke.

When they were alone at the pier's edge, Melissa and Joe ignored the slapping sounds of the sea. Looking instead into each other's eyes, they knew, right away, what their plans would encompass for the remainder of the day.

The walking tour of Key West, and other forms of outdoor activity, would be put on hold until tomorrow.

❧

It was late afternoon when they pulled up in front of the Cayo Hueso Motel. Not wanting to wait for a room service order, Joe and Melissa had already stopped at a local wine and spirits shop to purchase two large bottles of chilled champagne—as well as a few snacks.

After checking in as Mr. and Mrs. Jones, they toted their own bags to the room—then wasted no time in breaking out the stash of champagne. While they sipped, they also munched on wheat crackers, brie, and fresh strawberries.

For the next twenty minutes, Melissa and Joe sat on the floor of their room, cushioned by a deep pile carpet. After consuming a suitable amount of food, chased by bubbly, both of them seemed extremely loose and comfortable with each other.

They were smiling and joking now, like the winners of a championship game who were lingering in the locker room long after their victory became official.

The champagne had the effect of producing a lilting, laughing tone in both their voices.

Soon they were looking eye-to-eye and holding onto each other's hands. Alternately, Melissa would pull Joe toward her, and then he would reciprocate, with a brief kiss punctuating every movement. They also took turns pretending that their bodies were limp. Still sitting, they would close their eyes, pivot on the floor, and then trust each other to provide a soft catch of the partner's head and torso.

Engaging in such joyous frolic reminded Melissa of her grade school playmate, Clarissa. She and Clarissa were drawn together as friends, most likely, because others in their class would always poke fun at how their names were perfect rhymes. She could still see and hear the bratty little boys in third grade as they distorted their faces grotesquely and shouted, "Melissa-Clarissa, Melissa-Clarissa."

Melissa and her friend would often dance together, assume the roles of homemaking mothers, play patty cake, or just hold each other by the hands and sway, as Joe and she were doing right now.

Suddenly, in the midst of one of her giggles, Melissa sensed Joe's curly-haired head resting on her chest. He started nibbling on the large red stripe of her blouse. And, within seconds, Melissa could feel a pleasurable hardening beneath that blouse.

She placed her head against a pillow and grasped her arms around Joe's massive back. Then she began to experience a powerful warmth and comfort as his hand slowly started to caress the front of her body, in an exhilarating, circular motion.

The deep hum of pleasure that Melissa exhaled was a natural response. It was also, however, a signal to Joe that he needn't stop.

"Ooh, that's good," Melissa mumbled, quietly, close to Joe's ear.

Then, deftly, he slid his left hand under her blouse, massaging her bare, taut tummy before edging his fingers slightly higher, to an area where, on most days, Melissa would have been wearing a bra.

Swiftly, his lips moved to hers, commencing a tender kiss. Their tongues met, darting about inside their coupled mouths, seemingly in rhythm now with Joe's hands, which were passionately squeezing the soft erogenous zone of Melissa's bust line.

They were strong hands, hardened, she surmised, through the endless gripping of gun barrels, nightsticks, and squad car steering wheels. The very thought of this somehow made Melissa even more excited.

By now, Melissa's mind had begun to wander somewhere among her long forgotten teenage fantasies. Her womanly desires for Joe were transcending all vestiges of pure thought and proper instinct. At moments like these, she realized, the basic cravings of hunger, thirst, and logical reasoning are like badly beaten also-rans in a long distance foot race.

Melissa wanted dearly to be able to respond—by touching—to Joe's signals of desire. She reached for his belt buckle, flipped it open, and slid her right hand downward alongside his thigh, skin touching skin.

Compared to Brady, he had much stronger muscles on his legs. There were fewer strands of hair, she thought, but they were smoother to her touch.

Meanwhile, using both his hands in what seemed like one quick motion, Joe proceeded to grasp at the elastic of Melissa's skirt and panties, yanking downward. He eased his reclining body toward hers and then pulled her clothing skyward over the tips of her outstretched feet.

Tossing this bundle aside, he then used his tongue to tickle her slowly along the upward reaches of her knees.

"I need this, Joe, I need this oh-so badly," she told him.

After he gently lowered her legs to the carpet, Joe removed his trousers and briefs. He could tell now that she was ready, but he continued with the foreplay.

When Joe felt Melissa starting to tremble, he pressed himself, full length, on top of her. He planted a multitude of kisses on her lips, forehead, cheeks, and nose.

It was soon after they had become one that Melissa, uncharacteristically for her, seemed to begin an immediate climax. As she felt Joe's warmth envelope her, she lost all sense of time and location. She was unaware that the tips of her fingers were digging deeply into his strongly muscled back.

How many more times, Melissa wondered, would she stare blankly at white ceilings while being covered by this gentle yet muscular man? And how many more times would she sigh inwardly, and scream outwardly, with such consummate delight?

For several minutes after his release, neither of them seemed able to move so much as an eyebrow. Joe seemed to have used every last bit of strength in his successful efforts to please. And though Melissa still tingled with a special excitement, the day's activities, both indoors and out, had rendered her as exhausted as her newfound lover.

With heads now resting on each other's shoulders and their breathing still heavy, they clung together tightly, like two inseparable spoons stacked in a drawer full of silverware.

Eventually, Joe stood. Then, reaching down confidently for Melissa's hand, he led her over toward the king-sized bed.

After sliding themselves feet-first beneath a summery blanket, they caressed and pushed their lips together for one more kiss, summoning sleep.

Chapter 6

Paul's generosity continued.

Mary Ann and the girls selected new wardrobes during an all-day shopping spree in Philadelphia. As well, five new beds were delivered to Mary Ann's apartment, replacing the beach chairs.

The good times increased, too. The girls always looked forward to those evenings when Paul would take his new "family" out for dinner. As a group, they were adventurous when ordering from their menus—taking foods they had never before eaten, such as lobster and veal, and allowing each of their sisters to share a taste.

During one of Mary Ann's weekly visits to Paul's house, she took snapshots of every room so that she could show them to her daughters.

In the early part of May, Paul announced that he would be taking Mary Ann and the girls on a trip during the upcoming Memorial Day weekend.

"We'll be going to Ocean City, New Jersey, in about three weeks," Paul shouted, like an enthusiastic coach. "Will everybody be ready for the beach and the boardwalk?"

Although Mary Ann knew she would enjoy the intimacy that would be part of a weekend alone with Paul, she was glad the girls were coming along. She realized that they would have fun, but she was also somewhat relieved that sex between her and Paul would be impossible—since the kids would be staying in the same hotel suite.

In the back of her mind, Mary Ann always feared getting involved with yet another man who would demand sex constantly. Her ex-husband terrified her with his non-stop need for sex. In comparison, she now had a degree of freedom, living the life of an unmarried woman, with no live-in lover. Before Paul came into her life, she would "stray," as she put it, only once or twice a year.

When she was about ten years old, Mary Ann had her breasts fondled by one of her uncles, but she never told her parents about the incident. In the intervening years, she purposely excluded from her memory all thoughts of male family members, possibly blocking the recollection of additional incidents with the same uncle.

The child abuse in her past, Mary Ann believed, may be the reason she never experienced orgasms such as those she had read about or been told of by other women.

"I've never screamed during sex," Mary Ann admitted to Paul, "and I probably never will."

The boat ride on the Sunday before Memorial Day was the highlight of the entire weekend—as far as the girls were concerned. Five miles off the coast of Ocean City, they had their first experience with deep-sea fishing.

All told, their group boated two dozen sea bass, a scattering of sea robins and junkfish, and three small flounder.

The next day, their visit with "Lucy The Elephant" excited Mary Ann even more than it did the kids.

"Lucy," an imposing, three-story-high former hotel adjacent to the beach, was constructed in the shape of an elephant. Inside were antique slot machines that dispensed commemorative coins for every win. With a total investment of six dollars, Mary Ann was able to coax the machines into giving up four of the large, elephant-decorated coins—one for each of her girls.

Whenever they walked the boardwalk that weekend, Mary Ann and the girls would collect armfuls of stuffed animals—as a result of playing wheel spins, coin toss games, and assorted carnival teasers. Paul tried his hand, too, but without any luck.

Melissa was proud of the pink flamingo she won by knocking three bottles off a stand with a single pitch of a softball. The operator of the game tried to give her a larger stuffed flamingo, but Melissa had insisted on the smaller version.

"He has a sad face, Mommy," Melissa commented. "I'll make him happy."

At the conclusion of their vacation, during the long drive home, the girls were busy with their drawing and crayon coloring in the back of Paul's new station wagon. At least two of Mary Ann's girls seemed to have legitimate artistic ability.

"Their art work seems excellent," Paul noticed, "but it would probably be better if they could spend more time reading books. When I was in high school, my favorite English teacher always told our class, 'The dummies draw, and the smart kids read.'"

"When I was in high school," Mary Ann reacted, "my best subject was art. My favorite teacher thought I had a future as a commercial artist. But I never followed through on it. Maybe if I had, I wouldn't need to work as a weekend cashier to make ends meet, and I'd have more time to spend with my family."

Immediately, from embarrassment, Paul felt a blush. He was hoping, however, that his sunburn could hide it. He made a silent vow to make up for his insensitive remark as soon as possible.

⚭

Daybreak in Key West was instant warmth. To Melissa, the breeze that pushed its way through the open window felt like a tingling, toasty air current—the kind that a heating vent spews into a room during a mid-winter's day in Philadelphia, returning the wiggle to snow-frozen toes.

When they awoke on the bed, Melissa and Joe were still entwined, arm-in-arm. The absence of clothing led them to a logical, natural response—and so, they made love once again.

During this tender intermingling, Melissa felt overcome with passion. It was, she felt, her turn to steal the lead from Joe. And, like a dancer who can encourage a partner into the most memorable of moves, Melissa was coaxing Joe to a top-rate, all-star performance.

It was as if they were a medal-winning pairs team in Olympic ice-skating. They did nothing to impede each other. Those few imprecise movements went unnoticed. They were a positive complement, like the right wine with the right food.

While Melissa knelt, perched atop Joe, her tongue painted tiny circles under his ears, below his chin, and then from one side of his chest to the other.

Pulling him over on his side, she then reached around his body and used her left hand to massage the muscles in his back, pressing his torso tightly to hers with every movement of her pulsating fingers.

Deftly, she then moved her head toward the lower part of his body.

Alternately, she rubbed her face along the sides of both his massive legs.

Soon, Melissa and Joe were once again consummating their love, swaying to a rhythm that they alone had chosen.

Before long, their bodies were satisfied, having quenched this morning thirst for love—and for each other.

In time, Melissa and Joe resumed their normal breathing. And as do even the gods and goddesses of love, they turned their thoughts away from romance and toward the world that lay before them—on the streets of Key West.

While they showered and then packed, Joe reminded her that she was only about ninety miles away from the shores of Cuba, which was the next great land mass directly south.

"If I were a native of Key West," Melissa philosophized, "I'd want to get into a boat as often as possible and ride out in the water, as far west of here as I could. I guess I'm talking day trips, for sunshine, swimming, and fishing. I'd have to go at least once a week. Otherwise, if I didn't, I'd feel as though I were trapped. Living here—at the absolute end of Highway One—would be like being pinned, psychologically, against an invisible wall—with the only other way out a retreat back to Miami."

"You're right," Joe noted. "It probably would be restrictive. Aside from Hawaii, this is as far south as you can get in the United States. And you've got to go a long ways west of here before you see the shores of Texas. Maybe that's why the natives of Key West, knowing that they're at land's end, so to speak, are always in what seems like constant motion."

"Exactly," Melissa interrupted. "I noticed that yesterday. Even when we were driving on the side streets, away from the tourist areas, there were crowds of people on the sidewalks—pedestrian traffic jams."

"That's what rats do in cages, or what people do when they're arrested for the first time," Joe added. "I've seen it in my work. When a guy with no criminal record gets jailed, and he's inside the lockup, waiting to get bailed out, he'll walk around constantly, from one end of the cell to the other. And, once in a while, he'll stick his nose right through the bars—on top of the keyhole—hoping to get out of jail the exact instant the guard opens the door.

"Say, we're getting kind of negative here, aren't we?" Joe laughed.

Melissa followed with a chuckle of her own.

Soon, as they were leaving the room to check out, Joe advised Melissa to take along a sweater to wear later that evening, because the breezes on Key West are stronger than those on Islamorada.

"I think I'll pass on bringing the sweater," Melissa answered, giving Joe a hug. "Your warmth will be enough."

ॐ

In the center of town, at Mallory Square, they boarded the "Conch Train," a fifty-passenger, open-air tram. It came complete with soft seat cushions and a talkative guide. The tram was scheduled to take them past some of the island's more unusual attractions.

"What's your favorite color?" Joe asked, as soon as they had jumped on board.

"Aside from your eyes?" Melissa whispered. "Well, I've always been fond of pinks, yellows, and different shades of blue. I'm sort of a nervous, antsy person, and pastels seem to have the power to put me in a relaxed frame of mind."

"Well, our first tram stop will be at one of the old Martello Towers. These were originally the military forts that were built on the corners of the island to protect against an attack by sea—during the Civil War. Just a few years ago, the fort farthest from downtown was converted into a public flower garden. If I remember correctly, pinks and yellows bloom in abundance almost all year long."

Melissa's first reaction when she saw this huge fort-cum-flower-garden was that the once intimidating stone façade seemed to blend now, in an eye-pleasing manner, with the expansive covering of omnipresent bougainvillea, hibiscus, and wild orchids.

"It looks like a mix of the good and the bad, war and peace, the calm and the hectic," she effused. "Sort of like a statement that promotes non-violence. When I see flowers dominating a military fort, it's like when the nose of a cannon is propped straight up and turned into a flower planter. It tells me that peace has conquered war—that we are celebrating the death of guns."

When she had finished with this speech, Melissa remembered that Joe, being a policeman, might have differing views.

"Well put," he nodded. "But don't forget, I'm kind of proud that policemen like me are called keepers of the peace."

"That's true," Melissa admitted. "I guess the guns and peace thing could be a sensitive point to policemen. One shouldn't assume that the terms 'peace' and 'police' are mutually exclusive."

The next attraction along the route of the Conch Train was Ernest Hemingway's house on Whitehead Street. The building itself and the fenced grounds are now considered a national historic landmark.

Hemingway lived in Key West with his second wife, Pauline, from 1928 until 1940.

During its heyday, the house, which sits on one of the high water points of the town, was the biggest and most luxurious private residence in all of Key West.

"Don't think that it was Hemingway's money that built the house," Joe cautioned, as he and Melissa walked through an outside garden. "His wife was extremely rich, and even though Ernest had written a few of his best-sellers already, like *To Have and Have Not*, he could never have afforded this place on what he earned. Take the swimming pool, for example. It was the first in-ground pool ever built in the Florida Keys. It cost almost as much as the house, because the hard coral foundation had to be blasted out with dynamite. The mass of coral, being buried so close to ground level throughout the island, is the reason that most houses in the Keys don't have basements."

Melissa was delighted by the bevy of cats living at Ernest's house. Domestic short hairs of every possible color combination took turns brushing their bodies alongside her legs. A tiny, longhaired, tortoise-shell white was particularly friendly and affectionate.

"There must be close to a hundred here," she giggled, as she stopped to pet what seemed like every one of them.

"Hemingway loved cats," Joe smiled. "You'll notice that some of them have an extra toe on each of their front paws—a mutant strain.

"And since Hemingway liked to frequent the rowdy neighborhood tap rooms on an almost nightly basis, the locals tell the story that even his cats are predisposed to being better barroom brawlers—thanks to that extra claw."

The sunny but cool weather on Key West made Melissa wish she could stay for longer than just a day. The wide expanses of sand on the south side of the island were home for hundreds of multicolored beach chairs, looking like spring flowers sprouting wildly in the middle of a field.

"It's beautiful here, Joe, and it even has a little bit of class to it, what with the ethnic restaurants, the playhouse, and all of the museums. Key West also appears to have quite a few nightspots."

"You're right," Joe admitted. "The word, for want of something better, is culture—with a splash of night life. Key West has the same warmth and cool breezes that Islamorada has, but Islamorada's allure ends with the setting of the sun. Islamorada is peace and quiet at night. In Key West, with all the bars and clubs, there never seems to be a distinction between night and day—the action keeps right on going."

The last stop for the Conch Train was at the Key West Aquarium. And thanks to an aquarium host who was extremely knowledgeable, Melissa learned as much as possible about the sea life that inhabits the Keys. When the guide plucked a live, two-foot-long shark from one of the tanks and walked through the crowd, letting the tourists pet the beast's belly, Joe reached for his camera.

And when Melissa's turn came to place a hand on the shark, her pose was far from flattering.

"I got a good one of you and Jaws," Joe wisecracked. "And when we get this one developed, it will be a case of who looks more frightened, you or the shark."

∞

After a brief shopping spree in the stores on Mallory Square, during which Melissa bought a tee shirt bearing the air-brushed colors of a calico cat, it was time for dinner.

The restaurant that Joe had selected was called The Harbor's Bounty. Located near the boat docks on the north end of the island, it provided two fantastic views—one of the fishermen returning to port with their daily catch and another of the brilliant orange sun as it set on the Gulf of Mexico.

Throughout a dinner that was highlighted by conch fritters and crab claws, Joe and Melissa both exuded an outward calm that was half comfort at having spent a relaxing day in the sun and half contentment at having had the pleasure of one another's company.

"A day in Key West ends in a blaze of glory, doesn't it?" Melissa noted, gesturing skyward toward the searing fireball that was gradually disappearing on the horizon. "The sun kind of shimmers, like it's shining through a haze, but there is no haze."

"In Key West, we're closer to the sun," Joe reminded. "Remember, the equator is nearer to here than it is to Philadelphia."

After a dessert of key lime pie topped with whipped cream, Joe sprang a surprise on Melissa.

"There's a greyhound track just east of here, over the next bridge—on Block Island. Have you ever been to the dog races?"

"No, never have."

"Good, then maybe you'll bring us a bit of beginner's luck."

The Key West Kennel Club, as it was called, was vastly unlike those few horseracing tracks that Melissa had visited in the northeastern states. The grandstand building was a tiny, weathered wooden structure, while the racing surface itself encircled a small lake.

The greyhound races attracted only about five hundred patrons per night, but the racetrack's lack of size seemed only to add to its charm.

The sound of barking dogs greeted them as they drove into the sparsely filled parking lot. Walking near them as they headed toward the admission gates was a dog handler—leading two muzzled greyhounds.

"Those dogs have nice bodies," Melissa giggled. "Thin at the hips and wide at the chest—very sexy."

"I know that you're basically a cat person," Joe commented, "but I've always been partial to the running greyhounds. It's in my blood, I guess. My Uncle Steve, whom I've mentioned to you before, has always been a most avid racing fan.

"Back when I was a kid, Uncle Steve took me to the dog races in New England and to the thoroughbred races in New Jersey. He believed that there's something about the outside of a racing animal that turns on the inside of a man. And it's true.

"I really get excited when I see a dog or a horse competing in a race. Also, the racing sport itself is a great form of escapism. Whenever I'm at a racetrack for a few hours, I forget all about the nagging problems that are part of living from day to day."

"I'd like to meet this uncle of yours. He sounds interesting. Do you and he bet a lot of money on the dogs and horses?"

"I guess you'd call Steve a big bettor, but for me, I'm just a two-dollar guy on most races. Sometimes I'll splurge, though, and throw down a five or a ten."

Melissa's beginner's luck surfaced immediately. By selecting a dog solely on the basis of its name, she scored with her initial bet, collecting five dollars and sixty cents when Silverliner won the first race. She was unsuccessful, however, with two-dollar bets in both the second and third races.

"It's pretty here, Joe, with the lights reflecting off the lake and the way the stars and the moon get brighter as the evening goes on. The cool breezes feel good, too, after a day in the sun.

"I wonder if gambling on dogs and horses is as bad as all the moralists would lead us to believe?"

"I think that daily lotteries are a bigger problem nowadays," Joe interjected. "With so many states jumping on the bandwagon, those fifty-cent lottery tickets are available to just about everyone.

"Grandmom can buy a fistful of lottery numbers on her way to the corner store when she picks up the bread and milk.

"No, compared to horse and dog racing, the lotteries are much more pervasive. To lose money at a track, you've got to go out of your way to do it.

"Also, when you look at the casinos, that form of gambling is much more harmful. Casinos even extend credit to their patrons; racetracks don't."

Turning to the action in front of her, Melissa couldn't resist making a comment that was disparaging of canine IQ.

"After a while, you'd think the dogs would learn," she noted, "that the mechanical rabbit they're chasing is not what they think it is."

"Typical comment about the intelligence of dogs, coming from a cat person," Joe laughed. "Don't worry, if you lose a few more bets, you'll stop believing that the dogs are the dumbest ones here."

⚮

The long journey back to Islamorada provided another spectacular view, despite the absence of sunlight. On the superstructures of each of the many highway bridges were small red and green lights that lifted skyward, competing with the stars.

"It's just like the holiday season in Philadelphia," Melissa beamed. "I love to watch those tiny blinking lights on the trees that line the sidewalks.

"Here in the Keys, it's even neater. Looking at the tops of the bridges is like seeing giant Christmas trees from the north that have been replanted in the middle of the tropics."

Joe dominated the conversation during the traffic-free drive. And from the content of his comments, Melissa was acutely aware that he seemed genuinely interested in her future plans. She was unquestionably thrilled that someone she actually cared for was in the process of pursuing her.

"We'll have to go to the races again when I come up to visit you," Joe insisted. "And you'll have to show me some of the restaurants you like in Philly."

Inwardly, Melissa was ecstatic at Joe's roundabout yet possessive remarks. There seemed to be no reason at all now to think that he considered her as merely a means to a one-night stand.

"Uncle Steve's going to like you, just wait. He'll fall in love with you as soon as he sees you."

The horror stories about broken romances that she had heard from her female acquaintances on so many different occasions didn't seem pertinent at all as far as she and Joe were concerned.

Melissa was crossing her fingers now, hoping she needn't heed the tales of Natalie, Ruth, and Jennifer regarding those nameless, heartless men who had disappeared from their lives after a night or two of recreational sex.

"We'll have to come back to Key West again," Joe told her. "Once or twice a year, at least."

Melissa smiled, and despite her best efforts, drifted off to sleep safely snuggled against Joe's shoulder.

Chapter 7

Mary Ann and Paul quickly developed a favorite pastime—attending the races at the nearby track where Paul's horses were stabled.

On an average of about two evenings every week, from about 7 to 11 p.m., they would sit in the same area of the grandstand, in the same seats. Now and then they'd walk to the betting windows to place a wager, but most of the time they'd just sit and talk to each other, talk to fans sitting nearby, and experience the joy of seeing horses run. Paul noted, and Mary Ann agreed, that a summer's night at the races had all the "getting acquainted" advantages of the bar scene, but without the booze and without the noise. There was a certain harmony among all the factors that led to this allure.

"I've found out a lot about you just from sitting here and talking," Mary Ann told Paul one evening. "You said you were astounded by the number of guys you see at the track who have tattoos on their arms. But before I met you, I thought all men had tattoos. I was surprised when you swore to me that you never had even one."

"I swear, never."

"And what about laundromats? Remember that old woman, the one who wore four sweaters and was carrying those big shopping bags? She sat down in front of me, and all she talked about were horses and laundromats. I think it's amazing that you've never been to a laundromat. I've gotten to know some of my best friends at laundromats. They're great places for women to chitchat. I've even met men at laundromats."

"And I've learned a lot about you, too, M.A.," Paul countered, "especially from the people-watching we do when we're here. Remember on that rainy, cool night when I pointed out the kid who was wearing the wild, five-color, psychedelic jacket? I asked you if you'd ever have the guts to wear a coat that looked like a slapdash abstract painting."

"I remember," Mary Ann admitted. "You wanted to know if I'd wear something like that to make a statement, but I said there would be nothing symbolic about it, that whether I'd wear the jacket or not would depend on whether it felt warm."

Occasionally, one or two of the girls would tag along when Mary Ann and Paul went racing. To the children, though, racetrack attendance was only secondary entertainment. The real fun was the visit, before the races, to the stabling area. This activity was much more to the girls' liking. For while they'd walk from barn to barn, they would feed carrots to the horses and offer table scraps to the many cats who roamed the grounds.

Mary Ann said she should have known that the lure of the friendly felines would gradually overpower the girls. Melissa and Annie were the co-conspirators who kidnapped a chubby little calico from Barn R on a warm, muggy night in August.

"If I'd have been aware that they were kidnapping four cats in one, I'd never have let it happen," Mary Ann reflected.

"But I'm sure it turned out all right," Paul laughed. "There's no way the girls could have known that Puff was pregnant when they ran off with her. It was a good experience for them, watching Puff give birth."

The racetrack wagering that Paul and Mary Ann engaged in always seemed to follow the same pattern. Paul would make $20 bets three or four times a night, and Mary Ann would risk $2 or $4 on most of the races. Paul would give her $30 at the beginning of each evening, and Mary Ann would either lose it all or turn that $30 stake into $100 or so.

Paul learned even more about Mary Ann's character when she hit for $60 on the first race one night in early September and offered Paul half of the money right away. A week later, a $4 bet she made returned a whopping $150.

"Wow, it takes me a week to make this much at my job," she screamed, waving the winning ticket in front of Paul's nose. "Now I can rescue some of my layaways.

"Oh, I forgot," she continued, looking straight at Paul. "You might not know about stuff people can buy on layaway."

"If you ever hit a really big bet, M.A., several thousand, for example," Paul asked her, "what would you do with it?"

"I'd buy the girls the best art supplies I could find and sign them up for the special classes at Allentown Art Museum," Mary Ann answered, without blinking. "Then I'd put some money down on a new car. All of my life I've never owned a new car. And then, if there was any money left over, maybe I'd treat myself to a washer and dryer. But if I did that, then I wouldn't be able to drive my new car over to the laundromat."

On his next bet, Paul won $500 on Greystoke, a long shot he would have overlooked if Mary Ann had not pointed it out. After picking up his winnings, Paul turned to Mary Ann, handing her the money, and said, "I want you to have this money, Mary Ann, and buy the girls those art supplies and art lessons. I'd like to think I was the first patron of a budding, American, female Picasso."

_∽

On the following morning, a certain inevitability occurred, as it does with all vacations—the going home.

Melissa's plane was due to depart Miami later that evening. In the interim, she and Joe would share one last day with each other in the Florida sun.

The plan for the morning of departure was to leave Islamorada right after breakfast, motor to Miami, and spend the last few fleeting hours in Florida's largest city.

"You'll like Miami," Joe touted. "It has its own special kind of charm. For lack of a better description, it's sort of like an air-conditioned Atlantic City. Big hotels, big money, and a sprinkling of ethnic neighborhoods."

"I'm really going to miss Islamorada," Melissa told him, almost with a tear in her eye. "The whipping of the wind through the palm fronds and the quiet comfort that comes over me every time I walk on the beach will be difficult to forget. I'll also miss waking up every morning and seeing the egrets, the pelicans, and the roseate spoonbills fishing for their breakfasts in the shallow waters.

"Ever since yesterday I've been psyching myself up to leave. And perhaps I really am getting a little homesick for Philadelphia. The suitcase full of dirty laundry tells me it's time to go home.

"But there is one thing I can't do when I'm in my house," Melissa noted, pointing to Joe and smiling a bit wistfully.

"While I'm lying in bed at home, trying to fall asleep, I can't listen to the ocean."

"Someday soon, my lady," Joe commiserated, with his arm around her shoulder, "there'll be another time, another dance."

&

Joe led the two-car convoy, driving his personal automobile, not the police cruiser. And Melissa kept her rental a constant six lengths behind him as they traveled along two-lane Route 1.

The traffic was minimal until they reached Key Largo, where the road split briefly into a four-lane configuration.

Once they passed over the drawbridge at Grouper Creek, there was still about a half-hour stretch to go of narrow, deserted macadam—with highly visible water on both sides. Melissa hoped that the sea level was already at its highest tide, because, during several brief moments, the glistening waters to the right and to the left seemed to be higher than her shoulders.

At one point during the drive, Melissa noticed the remnants of an old Burma Shave advertising sign perched in the hard coral just off the highway.

"All of Islamorada was like one big step back in time," she told herself. "The charm of the entire Florida Keys is in being able to get a taste of rural America as it was in the 1950s, or maybe even the 1940s, without having to travel somewhere far inland in the Midwest, hundreds of miles from the nearest ocean."

Joe had planned a brief respite on the way to the Miami airport—a visit to the sprawling grounds of the Everglades National Park.

For about twenty minutes of travel time to the west of Route 1, through vast fields of sprouting tomato plants, they zoomed their way toward a meeting, face-to-face, with Florida's famed alligators.

"This is definitely farm country," Melissa told herself, surveying the acres of tomatoes and what she perceived to be an occasional field of green peppers.

She was charmed at the sight of the single-engine crop dusters that flew but a few feet over the roadway, spreading white, artificial clouds that covered the vegetables.

When she and Joe arrived at the visitors' center, they saw that there were only a handful of other tourists in the park.

"This is a good luck stop for us," Melissa told Joe. "I just saw a cat walking behind those bushes. Cats are always good luck."

Melissa was especially glad to be able to step out of her air-conditioned car and into the warming sun again—with Joe at her side. She wished, however, that she could be wearing a comfortable pair of shorts and a tank top instead of the prim brown skirt and high-collared, matching blouse that she called her "take an airplane outfit."

The park itself provided two main paths. The first was much like a boardwalk, the kind that made Atlantic City famous. This version stretched for about a half-mile, in a huge circle, through and just barely over the lush green swampland.

Melissa was bending over the railing when she took her first look at a live alligator. It was swimming, ever so stealthily, through what appeared to be shallow water.

At one point, a group of three other alligators, much smaller, congregated directly under the boardwalk. They were vocal, too, making the guttural sounds that dogs emit when they expect to be fed.

"I think they're barking," Melissa told Joe.

"They are."

"If I close my eyes," she joked, squinting, "it sounds like the Key West greyhound track."

"You'd better walk quickly, my dear," Joe counseled, "it must be feeding time."

The second of the parkland walkways coursed through an overgrown tropical jungle. Soon after entering this pristine setting, Melissa and Joe beheld a sunken grove filled with wide-bodied divi-divi trees that lay sprawled before them, leafless and sporting outgrowths of gnarled wood that gave the appearance of a school of giant octopi brandishing their menacing tentacles.

Multicolored flowers were plentiful on both sides of the path, as were towering patches of bamboo.

"It looks like an immense floral arrangement, designed in heaven," Melissa offered, "absolutely breathtaking.

"The way the long-stemmed flowers are bunched together, hanging over both sides of the path, makes it look spooky. I expect to see the eyes of a lion cub peering out at me."

A brief, five-minute walk took them to the far reaches of the path. And except for the chirping of an occasional bird and the whispering of the warm air as it whistled through the scrub pines, they were alone.

Melissa and Joe, arm-in-arm now, were soaking up the solitude of the forest and luxuriating in the warm feelings generated by two people who truly care for each other.

"If I could go back in time and be twenty years old again," Melissa revealed, "I'd attack you immediately, and we'd be lying in the grass under the shade of that tree."

Without saying a word in response, Joe brought her closer to him and hugged her gently. Quite naturally, they stopped to kiss.

Rubbing noses together, like two enraptured high schoolers on a first date, they pecked at each other's lips a number of times and then hugged, again, while swaying, ever so slightly, to the rhythm of the tropical breezes.

But before their minds, or their desires, could leap to any more erotic activity, they heard the sounds of oncoming footsteps. Muffled voices indicated the approach of children.

Within seconds, Melissa and Joe were smiling and saying hello to their fellow tourists, a family of four.

"Nice day, isn't it?" the father of the group offered, as he held onto the tiny hand of his blonde and toddling daughter. "Makes you kind of wish you could live forever."

"No, not quite," Melissa thought, as she clutched Joe's hand even tighter. "LOVE forever would be more like it."

∽

In less than an hour after leaving the Everglades, they had arrived at the airport in Miami. The first step was to turn in the rental car. Also, Melissa made it a point to check her luggage—far in advance of the flight's departure time.

Soon afterward, she and Joe were headed off for a bit of last-minute sightseeing.

They visited for a while at the famed flamingo exhibit in the nearby town of Hialeah. Although the Hialeah racetrack itself was closed and would not begin its yearly thoroughbred meeting until February, the exotic bird exhibit on the grounds was open all year round.

Hundreds of beautiful pink birds make their home alongside the racetrack's two man-made lakes.

Occasionally, a group of flamingos will soar skyward, flying off for a few seconds in a wave of color before landing effortlessly on their long, spindly legs.

"They look like one big pink cloud, don't they, flitting across the sky?" Melissa commented, "as graceful in the air as they are on the ground."

"The fact that they're pink sets them apart, I guess," Joe noted. "It makes them unusual. No one would care if they were gray, or if they were blackbirds, or pigeons."

"Sort of like blue food, is that what you're saying?" Melissa countered. "That's why I always love to eat blueberries. They look so neat. And, really, there isn't any other food that's blue."

"No other food, you say?

"Hmmmm, now you've got me thinking," Joe admitted, deliberating. "Before the end of the day, I guess I'm going to have to come up with the name of another kind of blue food.

"Just you wait, lady. Just you wait."

☙

The final stop on their itinerary was at yet another of southern Florida's many wagering emporiums—the Miami jai alai fronton, where they relaxed over lunch.

"Horses, dogs, jai alai, they're all separation centers," Joe wisecracked, in reference, sarcastically, to the separation of money from wallets.

The game of jai alai, extremely popular in the Miami area, is of Basque origin, Joe told her.

Distantly similar to racquetball, it is played either as a series of singles matches, man against man, or in pairs, with two teammates doing battle against two other teammates.

Instead of a racquet, though, each player uses a wicker "cesta," a basket-like mitt strapped to the wrist. The ball, called a "pelota," is caught in the cesta and hurled toward a wall at speeds that can reach in excess of one hundred miles per hour.

Just as in tennis, the ball must be returned by an opponent before it bounces twice. Two bounces or a failure to catch results in a lost point.

"The word 'fronton' refers to the building in which jai alai is played," Joe explained. "Aside from animal racing of one kind or another, this is the only other sport in America that you can bet on—legally, that is."

Melissa enjoyed watching the games, seeing the short-sleeved, helmeted players jumping, running wildly, and literally climbing walls to return a steady series of difficult shots. The balls most often dropped were low, spinning volleys that hit the cestas and popped out.

Melissa also noticed that the "standing room only" section, with its fifty-cent admission charge, was jam-packed with fans. "Most all are men," she noted, while surveying this Miami crowd. "Cigars, gray beards, and rumpled baseball caps. From the looks of this group, yuppies aren't the targeted audience for jai alai."

"Definitely an older crowd," Joe said, "with few women."

"It's great fun to watch this game," Melissa beamed. "And everybody here seems to be really getting into it, what with all the loud yelling."

"Half of the cheers are in English," Joe added, "while the others sound like Spanish."

"I think I hear a third language," Melissa stated.

"What's that?"

"New York."

"Jai alai doesn't need betting to be fun," Joe believed. "All the players look evenly matched. There doesn't seem to be any need for scientific betting strategies. It's like playing a roulette wheel or putting money on a throw of the dice."

To spur Melissa's interest level even higher, Joe bought her a win ticket in the third game on the number eight player, Carlos.

"He's doing well, isn't he?" Melissa exclaimed, as she watched the action.

"Yes. He looks quick."

"Go, Carlos, go," she encouraged.

Near the end of his match, Carlos was only a single point away from a victory at betting odds of six-to-one. At that point in the action, he just barely missed an attempt to catch his opponent's tricky backhand shot, which had ricocheted, at a horrendous angle, off the back wall.

"He dropped it," Melissa screamed. "Oh, that was stupid. Really dumb. Did you see that? He just dropped the ball for no good reason."

"Tough luck."

"Don't buy me any more tickets," Melissa told Joe, half-jokingly. "Frustration like this is something I don't need."

∽

From their seats in plastic chairs at the airport departure gate, Joe and Melissa watched the sun begin its slow retreat from the sky.

The gradual dissipation of light seemed a bit symbolic. It was as if the gods were sending out a message saying, "The sunshine of your vacation is now setting. Your plane awaits you like Cinderella's fairy-tale carriage."

Melissa was now confident, though, that the new sunshine of her life, Joe Carlton, would not be disappearing over the dusky horizon.

"Two weeks, Melissa, that's all," Joe consoled her. "We'll be together again when I visit you at Christmas."

"But in Philadelphia, it won't be eighty degrees with sun and surf," she complained. "It'll be more like thirty degrees—with snow.

"You're going to have to bring a whole lot of sunshine with you inside your suitcases, Mr. Carlton, because I'm going to need it."

After they had kissed good-bye, Melissa turned to walk toward the crowd that was entering the jet way. It was a suntanned but sad-looking group. Some had carry-on bags that held tennis racquets. It seemed strange to see the occasional passenger who was wearing shorts while at the same time toting a heavy winter coat.

When Melissa turned to look back in Joe's direction, for one last time, she noticed that he was cupping his hands over his mouth and shouting. At first, she couldn't understand him.

"Bluefish," he intoned.

"What?"

"Bluefish."

After hesitating for a reflective half-second, Melissa responded, shaking her head in an obvious negative direction.

"Doesn't count! No way!" she screamed back at him, for all of the airport to hear. "Not really blue. Keep thinking."

Chapter 8

Mary Ann cooked the full-course Thanksgiving dinner, including the pumpkin pies baked from scratch. And as soon as the girls had finished doing the dishes, the family talk turned to Christmas.

Mary Ann remembered that just a year ago, she had taken a part-time job delivering morning newspapers—so she could accumulate a few extra dollars for Christmas. But even with the girls helping her, Mary Ann found that the Sunday papers were too heavy to carry. After just two weeks, she quit. Within days, though, she landed a sales clerk position three nights every week at a jewelry store.

"To get the jewelry job," she told Paul, "I first had to take a train up to Allentown, where they gave me a lie detector test. Of course I passed, but I always felt somehow 'dirty' at that job. I was relieved when I was able to quit."

As to Christmas traditions, one of Mary Ann's personal favorites was a visit to the Iris Club, a restaurant for which she held an eight-dollar yearly membership. She looked forward to taking Paul there and sharing another part of her life with this man who had become so important in all their lives.

"Steamed clams and beer, that's what I always get," Mary Ann smiled. "It'll be my treat. I only get to go there about twice a year. I used to waitress at the Iris back when Donald and I first got married. It was a nice place to work. My memory of the place and of the people I met gets better every year. Who knows, at the rate I'm going, when I'm in my eighties and dying, I might be praying for God to send me there."

While Mary Ann and Paul were dining at the Iris Club, she saw an old friend of hers, Debbie Eck. Debbie, also an ex-waitress, had since become a driver of tractor-trailer rigs. In a proud and no-nonsense manner, Mary Ann introduced Paul as her "fiancé." Debbie congratulated both of them and then stayed around for a while, reminiscing. Mary Ann fondly remembered those evenings when she and Debbie would drive into the woods near Manatawny Creek, "spotting" for deer with their flashlights.

The next bit of Christmas celebrating was at Paul's insistence: "A bus ride to Philadelphia for some Christmas shopping. We'll go on a Saturday. The girls will just love it."

Two weeks later, while their bus was on the expressway, nearing the center of Philadelphia, they heard the driver advise all passengers to "stay in your seats, because the traffic will get heavy."

And once they arrived, the pedestrian traffic proved even heavier. Despite being jostled occasionally in the crowds, the girls enjoyed their escalator ride to the top floor of Wanamaker's department store; they shopped; they ate huge soft pretzels purchased from street vendors; they did more shopping; and they walked along the Delaware riverfront, taking pictures of tugboats.

In one store alone, a curio shop called Past, Present & Future, Mary Ann spent close to half-an-hour browsing through the knickknacks.

Some of the people they saw on the streets of Philadelphia were unlike any the girls had ever seen in Pottstown. A strolling guitar player, a man wearing a skirt, and several panhandlers elicited gawks and giggles from each of Mary Ann's daughters.

Melissa was intrigued by a portable pulley that was transporting trash bags from a sixth-story window onto the bed of a pickup truck. She would have stayed at curbside for hours, watching the bags descend, if Paul hadn't promised he'd get her a library book that explains pulleys.

The onset of darkness brought with it a unique sleigh ride. Paul put the gang on a horse-drawn buggy, complete with fringe and bells, that pulled them through the brightly decorated historic district.

"Is it cruel to the horses, Mommy?" Melissa asked, as she sat in the front of the buggy, her hands and legs covered with a blanket provided by the driver. "We weigh a lot, especially with all the shopping bags we have. I hope the horses don't get tired of pulling us."

Later, while they waited to board their bus for the homeward trip to Pottstown, Paul bumped into a former business associate. Immediately, he saw his chance to return a favor to Mary Ann.

"My fiancée, Mary Ann," he voiced, affirmatively.

Soon, from the windows of the bus, they watched the moonlight reflecting on the Museum of Art and saw the Christmas lights on the boathouses along the Schuylkill River.

Mary Ann told Paul that when he introduced her as his fiancée, she seemed to get a sudden boost of self-confidence.

"It's hard to explain," she noted, squeezing his hand. "A feeling of worth, I guess. Thank you."

Christmas Day itself seemed warm and comfortable, an atmosphere amplified by the blinking lights from a real tree—always a must for the girls.

Paul's gifts to Mary Ann included a box full of art supplies, a watch, and a large wall calendar that featured horses running through open fields. "I usually buy my calendar after New Year's," Mary Ann laughed, "when they're on sale."

Paul was saving the biggest gift for last. In the meantime, he opened his own presents from Mary Ann and the girls, who had gone in together to get him a tool kit and a gold tie clip engraved with his name. From Paul, the girls received enough new clothes to be, without a doubt, the best-dressed students in their neighborhood.

The cats, too, were in line for gifts. Their catnip-filled toys were wrapped in paper that held the slogan: "Have a Purry, Purry Christmas."

Paul waited until the girls had gone to sleep before he took the small box from his jacket pocket.

"This is not an engagement ring, M.A., as you might think from looking at the size of it," Paul admitted. "But before you open it, I'm going to ask you to marry me. You don't have to give me your answer right away, but I want you to know that even if you turn me down, you can still have what's in this box. And if you agree to marry me, we'll pick out your engagement ring as soon as you're ready to go shopping for it.

"Also, there's something I need to share with you before you give me your answer. I'm afraid I haven't always been honest with you from the first day we met."

Mary Ann gave Paul a startled, questioning look. "Oh, don't worry," he continued, "I'm not secretly married or anything. What I need to tell you is that our meeting was not a coincidence. Father Stevens told me your story about finding my wallet. I know he promised not to, but I was so taken aback that my wallet was returned with all its contents fully intact, that I insisted he share the story of its finding.

"When he told me your story, I was overwhelmed by your situation. I have always been pretty lucky all my life. I've been fortunate enough to go to the right schools and find a job that pays me very well. True, my first wife died, and we never did have any children with whom I could share my life. But I never faced the kinds of adversity that you have, and I just wanted to meet you and understand how you could be so selfless.

"Of course, I thought we would just have a conversation, and I might be able to discover a way to help you get the credit you had been trying so hard to establish. But when I saw your face, and those of your little girls, I just knew that I wasn't going to walk away. You have taught me so much, Mary Ann, about what is important in life. And now, all I want to do is share the rest of my life with you and the girls.

"Now, without saying a word, please," he continued, "open the box."

"Your new car," the note inside the box read, "is the little red wagon parked next to mine. Merry Christmas, M.A.

"Love, Paul."

⬯

Melissa's radiant suntan, an uncommon wintertime sight in the Northeast, made her the envy of her Philadelphia friends.

And although she described the pleasure of Islamorada to all of her co-workers at the library and to all of those in her circle of acquaintance, she withheld any mention of Joe. Likewise, she said nothing about her dramatic rescue from the Seascaper's flaming fishing pier.

Melissa was hesitant, because she didn't want her classy lifestyle, super-educated friends to think that she was sex-starved. Being a recent divorcee, she might be accused of taking the first pants-wearing specimen who could flash a come-hither smile.

"But, then again, maybe I should be just as wary of men as those critics would be," she told herself, reflectively. "Perhaps I'm attracted to Joe because I'm lonely now. Or maybe, compared to Brady and his many faults, which I can see clearly now, any normal appearing male would look halfway decent."

However, the more Melissa thought about her budding new romance while she relaxed in these, her comfortable, homey surroundings, the more she became convinced that her interest in Joe was, indeed, the real thing.

The only person she did confide in regarding what she now considered to be a positive upheaval in her personal life was Cammie, her best friend. Melissa knew that Cammie, also a librarian, could always be depended upon for an honest, straightforward opinion.

"The thing that bothers me most," Melissa told her, "might be his lack of formal education. It might not seem like much now, but it could turn into a heavy problem. Could I be happy spending my life with someone who never advanced past high school?"

"Are you worried about his lack of a college degree more because your friends would think negatively of him," Cammie began, "or more so because you believe that eventually the different educational levels will cause you and Joe to break up?"

After a pensive few seconds, Melissa agreed that she had no qualms, at present, about educational levels causing them to split up somewhere down the road. She then thanked Cammie for her incisive analysis.

"You're right—I think," Melissa giggled. "I guess it's more my being a social animal than any doubts I might harbor about Joe. I know I love him, and I sincerely believe that he loves me, too. So, what other people think about him or what other people think about us shouldn't be a factor in our relationship. I'm just having an extremely hard time convincing myself that I shouldn't care two twits what other people's opinions might be."

"You said it—that's exactly the problem," Cammie emphasized. "Whether you fall in love with a mass murderer, with a Mafia drug dealer, or with the next squeaky clean president of the United States, it shouldn't matter. If you love a guy, everything else is immaterial.

"So, really, Melissa, there's nothing wrong with loving a policeman. Don't worry about your friends. Instead, worry about the one guy who's going to be your BEST friend.

"And stop thinking like a snob. Social class distinctions disappeared with the Model T. This isn't nineteenth-century England, and it isn't India. This is the United States of America."

For Melissa, there were moments during these two weeks without Joe that felt like two years.

Her day-to-day life seemed to be a continuum of rote motion: sleep, eat, work at the library, and spend an occasional evening with a friend. Sometimes she found herself staring at her plants, not even sure how she got in the room, or if she had watered them or not.

"I'll be ready for sex as soon as I see him," she told herself, "and I might not even care if it's safe."

In Melissa's battle to keep cheerful, Christmas shopping proved to be a welcome diversion. She even bought a gift for Joe's Uncle Steve, whom she knew she would finally get to meet come Christmas Eve.

"What better gift for a horse player than a wallet with plenty of space for winnings," Melissa thought, as she smilingly purchased a large, brown leather model with a small stitched "S" on the front.

Despite the random distractions, however, the expectation of Joe's holiday visit dominated her every waking moment.

Admittedly, Melissa was slightly apprehensive about having everything "just right for Joe." These feelings were tempered to a great degree, though, by the joy she experienced every day during that two-week period as she came closer and closer to a reunion with the man she had come to love.

When the time finally arrived for Joe's plane to land at Philadelphia International Airport, the extreme nervousness Melissa had exhibited during the past few days had, quite strangely, begun to subside. She was, in fact, proud of herself for being "almost calm."

And, as soon as their eyes met at Gate B-12, they walked toward each other as if in a trance, or guided by some supernatural bond. Joe's kiss, and his embrace, were warmly satisfying.

"I can never, ever, remember Brady kissing me for such a long time," Melissa told herself. "Brady's kisses were short and devoid of feeling. Joe's kisses, in comparison, are like bursts of sunlight on a beautiful spring day.

"I have no doubts right now that Joe is the guy I should have married so many, many years ago. I guess I should feel no regret, though. After all, Joe and I were different people way back then—when we were younger. Most likely, if we'd met in the past, there would have been no spark, no magic."

During the drive from the airport back to Melissa's house, they discovered that their own personal magic, born in the warmth of the Florida Keys, was still alive in frozen Philadelphia.

At the passing of every intersection, and at every curve in the highway, they looked, ever so briefly, at each other. The desire that had been dormant during their separation seemed once again strong. It was outdistanced abundantly, however, by love.

As soon as they pulled into Melissa's garage, with the automatic door closing behind them, they embraced. Almost without thinking, they slowly slipped into reclining positions on the front seat of the car.

After kissing and caressing each other in the most personal of places— their bodies warm with want, they suddenly stopped—at Melissa's urging. Then, hurriedly, she led Joe up the stairway to the kitchen.

Melissa hesitated briefly to greet Coke, her white alley cat, pausing just long enough to give the puss two quick pats on the head.

Next, they went out through another door and onto the enclosed, heated porch. Joe's luggage, left behind in the trunk of the car, would have to wait its turn.

Soon, they were standing alongside a soft and ample sofa in this warm, comfy enclosure. Lovingly, they began to undress each other.

Melissa began by unbuckling the belt on Joe's faded jeans. While she slid her hands down both his hips, he was busy opening the zipper on the back of her greenish-blue blouse.

Within seconds, their clothing sat in one common pile, catching the winter sunlight that was shining through a crack in the drawn curtains.

Effortlessly, Joe lifted Melissa onto the sofa, which had been prudently situated between various houseplants that were hanging from the ceiling and others that were tastefully perched on tabletops throughout what Melissa called her "flower room."

"Making love here, in the warmth of my favorite room, while the outside temperature is below freezing and snow flurries are landing on the sidewalk is the closest thing possible to sex in the summery outdoors," Melissa smiled to herself. "The spider plants, sweet olives, and begonias make me feel like I'm in the wilds of a jungle—being protected by the resident Tarzan."

"I need a few hibiscus and Norfolk pines," Melissa remarked, this time speaking to Joe while gesturing toward a group of nearby plants, "to remind me of Islamorada."

"Where's Islamorada?" Joe answered, as his lovemaking proceeded to the serious stage.

Melissa tried to laugh in return but couldn't, being hard pressed to keep her breath. She uttered nothing for the next few minutes, except for an occasional whimper of pleasure heard only by Joe and by Coke, who was sitting on one of the tables between a pachysandra and a philo-dendron—the miniature tiger in a miniature jungle—purring in concert with his mistress's sounds of satisfaction.

∽

The following morning, while they were still in bed, Joe was the first to bring up the subject of marriage.

"If you'll agree to have me, Melissa, I'd love for you to become my wife. Ever since we said good-bye to each other in Florida, I've done little else except think about you. It was never my idea to fall in love so quickly with someone—but I have. I think, too, that it's about time I said adieu to this beach boy image that's been part of me for so long now. I know that I started into it to escape the memory of Becky. But you have totally driven her from my mind. You've made me realize that Joe Carlton must eventually grow up. The fact that I love you so much makes me want to show you that I'm mature now—that I can succeed in anything I try—as long as you're right there with me."

Melissa, too, was not at a loss for words.

"I accept," she whispered, kissing him tenderly on his cheek.

"I almost asked you first," she admitted. "Back in Florida, when we talked about the possibility of marriage, I had this deep down feeling that you were the one guy I should never, never let get away."

"Now it's my turn to interrupt you," Joe insisted. "I want you to know that you don't have to worry about relocating to Islamorada to find a job.

I've decided that I'm going to be the one who relocates. With my experience in police work, I should be able to find plenty of leads right here in the Philadelphia area.

"And if I'm lucky," he cracked, "I might even find something that pays half as much as you make!

"The worst thing that could happen is that we'd have to move a few miles from here so that we'd be equal commuting distances from work. All you'll have to do in the meantime is put up with me until I find that job.

"Agreed?"

"I think," Melissa stated, forcefully, "that we've got ourselves a deal."

It was Joe's idea that they shop together for her engagement ring.

"Since a woman has to wear it all of her life," Joe believed, "she should get to pick it out."

They traveled to the downtown area of Philadelphia and browsed through several stores in an area called "Jewelers' Row."

On the way home, Melissa was wearing her diamond.

"Now I've got to tell all of my sisters," Melissa complained, though cheerfully. "Then I've got to call my mother and stepfather in California. And then I've got to show up at work and think of things to say when everyone congratulates me.

"And what about tonight?" Melissa continued, her voice hitting a higher note.

"When we're at the Christmas party with all of my co-workers, what will I say?

"The worst thing about all of this is that my friends will never tell me what they really think of you if they find out we're already engaged!

"If I could introduce you as a friend only and not as a fiancé, then I'd get some feedback a few days down the road."

"Then don't wear the ring, just for tonight," Joe suggested. "Make it easier on yourself. I don't mind."

"You're an angel," Melissa responded, kissing him again while she kept both her hands on the steering wheel. "But I'll feel funny if I don't have it with me.

"I know, I'll wear it on a necklace. It'll be out of sight, of course, but it'll still be close to my heart."

"You've got to promise me, though," Joe insisted, "that you'll let me know what your lady friends think of me. The gossip might prove to be interesting."

"Absolutely," Melissa countered, her eyes full of sparkle, "deal number two."

∞

Almost all of Melissa's co-workers showed up for the Christmas party. Some brought spouses or friends, while others came unattached.

From the forty-odd attendees, there were about thirty women, and since a majority of the library's employees were female, most of the men on hand happened to be involved in other professional pursuits.

Joe found it easy to talk to the guys. Rob, husband of one of the library administrators, once worked on a construction site in south Florida. Rob talked with Joe quite a bit, as did Hubert, a former Army M.P. who was the fiancé of Marcy, one of the newer librarians on staff.

Throughout the course of the evening, Melissa introduced Joe to what seemed to be just about everyone in attendance.

She was proud of him, and the smile on her face affirmed the feeling. His light blue sport coat and gray slacks accentuated his tan, yet Melissa admitted to herself that she missed seeing him in uniform.

"This is Joe Carlton," her standard description would start, "Islamorada's top detective."

Whenever he would exchange pleasantries with the women in the group, Joe recognized right away that these were all professional and well-educated types—with high IQs.

From foreign affairs, to modern art, to stock market options, the topics of conversation never touched on the trivial—nor did they lag.

At times, Joe felt like a prospective student who was being questioned by the faculty prior to his acceptance to some prestigious private school.

Luckily, he survived the grilling without falling flat on his high school diploma.

The only time he stumbled slightly was when Jane, also a reference librarian like Melissa, asked him if he preferred reading the English mystery writers as opposed to their American counterparts.

"I don't care for either," he answered. "Since I'm involved in so many mysteries in my police work, reading a mystery novel would be like taking a busman's holiday. I prefer instead," he lied, "to write poetry—on those rare occasions when I feel a need to escape from the workaday world."

Joe had failed to mention that the last poem he had written was when he was in his early twenties. But though poetry was an interest of his that he had ignored for so many years, that long-lost attraction to the writing of verse still served a purpose—as cocktail party chatter that could successfully uplift his cultural profile.

Later, when Joe cornered Melissa alone at the far end of the snack table, he asked her about Jane.

"I've never read any of those murder novels in my entire life," he admitted. "And Jane is the third person here that I've heard discussing the works of mystery writers."

"You're lucky I haven't introduced you to that tall redhead sitting at the bottom of the staircase," Melissa pointed, using her wine glass instead of a finger. "That's Kim Powell, who'd probably ask you your opinion of the sentence structure in Marcel Proust novels."

"It's your fault, you know," Joe added, kidding his fiancée. "You introduced me as a detective and not a policeman. Obviously, they think I'm a combination of Mike Hammer and Sergeant Joe Friday."

"More like Hercule Poirot, I should hope," Melissa giggled.

"Who?"

"You're my mystery man," Melissa cooed, biting Joe's ear, "you're my very own mystery man."

☞

Christmas Eve morning in Philadelphia presented a beautiful sight. From the window in Melissa's living room, she and Joe could see soft flakes of snow floating gently in the cold air and then melting imperceptibly as they hit the sidewalk and the street outside.

The Christmas tree that Melissa had decorated, prior to Joe's arrival, blinked its miniature, multicolored lights in as soothing a visual rhythm as the falling snow.

"For as far back as I can remember, the rule in our house always was that no presents get opened until Christmas Day," Melissa instructed. "And you're not allowed to shake the boxes either."

Melissa spent the pre-noon hours on Christmas Eve making obligatory but joyful phone calls—first to her mother and her stepfather at their retirement village, which was a few miles outside of San Diego, and then to each of her three sisters.

The phone calls were longer than usual because of Melissa's big, big news—her engagement. Dutifully, Joe stood alongside her during each call, waiting for his turn to say hello and to "look forward to meeting you soon." Melissa made it easier for him to relate to the voices he heard by propping up on a table large photographs of Mom, Paul, Denise, Annie, and Susan.

"This will give every one of them something to talk about from now until way after New Year's Day," Melissa told Joe, in a mischievous manner, after hanging up on the last of the calls. "They'll be burning up the phone wires talking to each other and cursing the busy signals that they themselves will be causing."

The balance of Melissa and Joe's Christmas Eve was to be spent visiting Uncle Steve, Joe's favorite uncle. Steve's house was about a forty-five minute drive from Melissa's—in southern New Jersey.

"He'll be someone that you'll never forget, Mel," Joe predicted. "If you want a rough idea of what Joe Carlton will be like thirty years from now, Uncle Steve is it. When I'm his age, I'll probably look like him and think like him.

"He's the only family I've had in a long time, Mel, until you came along."

☙

From the small county highway where they parked the car, Melissa and Joe had an up-close view of Uncle Steve's tiny, ranch-style home. The late afternoon scene came complete with a snow-covered picket fence and a billowing chimney. The house, bathed in white, looked like a painting that Ma and Pa Kettle would have hung over their sofa, the kind of artwork Melissa's trendy friends would probably have called "American Primitive."

The snow was about an inch deep now. It covered the lawn, the bushes bordering the property line, the stone-inlaid walkway, and the magnificent blue spruce that stood guard near the doorway—its sloping branches like the outstretched palm of a hand, offering welcome.

Greeting them at the front door, before they could even knock, was a round-faced, round-bellied man who looked like a Santa Claus without the suit and beard.

"Ha, ha, ha," he bellowed, loudly, forgetting that it was he who was tending toward deafness and not his visitors. "You're just like Joey said you'd be, pretty as a picture."

Uncle Steve, who had spent over fifty of his seventy-some years as a trainer of racehorses, called Melissa the "first winner that Joey has picked since Seattle Slew."

"This nephew of mine has finally learned that selecting a woman is like trading for a horse," Uncle Steve winked.

"Conformation is the most important factor," he added, staring at Melissa's hemline, "especially the shape of the legs."

After Uncle Steve had started up the fireplace and poured drinks for everyone, he and Joe traded blood-oath promises. They agreed to get together again the following spring, when nearby Garden State racetrack would be open for thoroughbred racing.

Next came an exchange about what each of them had been up to lately.

"Did a little hunting last week," Uncle Steve noted, "but I came back empty. The jackrabbits in these parts are just getting too fast for these old eyes of mine."

Melissa found herself staring into Uncle Steve's eyes as he talked. She marveled at their clear blue color and how much they seemed to match Joe's.

"The last fishing I did in Florida was back in November," Joe admitted. "I caught some yellowtail that were good eating, and I almost boated a fair-sized marlin. But at least I didn't let the big one get away," he added, nodding his head toward Melissa while gently squeezing her hand.

"I don't know much about librarians," Uncle Steve acknowledged, also gazing in Melissa's direction, "but I can see now that what I thought I knew was all wrong.

"One look at you tells me that there must be a lot more librarians in this world who don't wear horn-rimmed glasses or have their hair pinned up in a bun."

"Thank you for the compliment, Uncle Steve," Melissa interjected. "And if your nephew here keeps his promises, I'll be one more librarian who won't wind up as an unmarried old woman."

Uncle Steve, who prided himself on his cooking skills, prepared an outstanding sauerbraten entrée—complete with the red cabbage and spaetzles that Joe had told him were Melissa's favorites.

"Had to force myself to learn how to cook after my wife died twenty years ago," Uncle Steve remembered, his eyes now just a trifle wet. "From the time we were married until the time Sally died, she cooked every meal for us.

"I kind of wish she could come back, for just a little while, so she could see what a great cook I've become. She'd be proud of me, she would."

Melissa noticed that although Uncle Steve seemed to be looking in her direction constantly, throughout the evening, it was a compassionate, fatherly look, far from the lecherous stares she'd seen in other men. It was more like the gaze of a man who was trying to place the circumstances under which they may have met some fifty years prior.

"She has Aunt Sally's smile, doesn't she?" Joe offered.

"In spades, my boy," Uncle Steve replied, gulping down one final jigger of brandy, "in spades."

⬿

"You were right about him," Melissa announced, as they drove home slowly through the slightly deepening snowstorm. "Uncle Steve is just what I hope you'll turn into, Joe Carlton, when you become a senior citizen. He seems like the kind of man whose loving words could make an older woman feel just as sexy as a homecoming queen."

"Oh," Joe interrupted, "in case you haven't noticed, Merry Christmas, Mel."

"It is midnight, isn't it?" she replied.

"All of a sudden I'm realizing," she continued, somberly, "that on the day after Christmas, you'll be gone again."

"Only for three weeks. Besides, you have a lot of planning to do for the wedding. The date, primarily," Joe laughed. "And maybe by the time we meet again next month for our weekend tour of Atlanta, I'll have some answers to those resumes I'll have sent out."

"Thank you, Joe, for a wonderful Christmas," Melissa told him.

"It's only the first," Joe responded. "From here on in, I'm told, they get better."

Chapter 9

Mary Ann never considered turning down Paul's proposal. She was convinced now that she was going to spend the rest of her life with the kindest, most loving, and most considerate man she had ever known. She believed that she was truly in love for the first time in her life. She just couldn't believe the circumstances that brought them together. Finding that wallet was certainly her lucky day, even if she didn't get an immediate cash reward. Meeting Paul was more reward than she could ever imagine.

The one-carat diamond engagement ring that Mary Ann wore 24 hours of every day seemed to shine brightest on winter mornings—its simple solitaire setting unsullied by city slush or dusty, frozen winds.

"I like to look at my ring," Mary Ann told the girls, who had gathered at her feet to hear the story of Paul's proposal and how their life as a family would change in the near future. "When I stare at my ring and see how it sparkles, I smile. And when I smile, I'm in a happy, healthy mood."

In counseling the girls, Mary Ann told them to look upon Paul as their new father. "What he says goes, and what I say goes. Once we get married, we'll be equal. And we should also be equal while we're helping you girls to grow up into young ladies."

One thing the girls noticed about their mother was that she no longer spent her quiet moments alone reading merchandise catalogs. Since Paul had purchased so many new clothes for her, Mary Ann decided to leaf through a few women's magazines, looking for advice on how to dress more fashionably.

She bought copies of *Woman's Day*, *Good Housekeeping*, and *Family Circle*—searching for tips on clothing accessories and hairstyles. One of the articles that intrigued her was titled "Ultimatum Time." In it, the author tells her female audience that when a man enthusiastically courts a woman, he will probably propose marriage within six months of their first date. However, if the six-month point passes without a proposal, the author contends, then the woman who's involved in the relationship should give her guy a "marry me or else" ultimatum.

Mary Ann knew that she never could have given Paul such an ultimatum. In the event he hadn't proposed, she would have continued the relationship—without any complaints. "I can't imagine life without him," Mary Ann admitted. "If he were to leave me now, I'd be devastated. If something like that should happen, I'd probably look for distractions, right away—simple pleasures, like feeding chunks of bread to the ducks on Museum Lake or taking long walks in the rain—anything to help me forget.

"And the loss of Paul's financial support would hurt, too. The bills would be harder to pay, and instead of going to gourmet restaurants to taste alligator tail, shark steak, and escargot, I'd be back to cooking frozen fish cakes for the girls and myself.

"When Donald walked out on me, I hated him. And I vowed that I'd never give him a second chance, even if he begged me. The girls are just too precious to have their emotions exposed that way. No, I don't suppose I could give any man who abandoned me a second chance, not even Paul.

"It may be unusual, but of all the people I've known throughout my life, men are the only ones I've ever really hated. Even some men that I haven't known well at all I've hated. Yet, I don't think I've ever hated a woman.

"And I know that having been sexually molested by my uncle when I was a kid is only partially to blame for the way I feel. Down deep inside, I think I hate my father and my brother, too.

"I'll never forget, back when I was in the fourth grade, Pop and Tony killing my pet rabbit. Later, they told me that the soup I was eating was rabbit stew. Every time I see a rabbit now, I remember staring at the soup and hearing laughter.

"I guess if anything causes Paul to leave me, it'll probably be because he's well-educated, and I'm not. I realize that he's smarter than me, and I wonder how an intelligent man such as him would break off an engagement. Would he tell me face-to-face?

"Maybe I'll ask him what he remembers most about his old girlfriends. Then I'll get an idea of what he'd remember about me. And if I can keep adding to that store of pleasant memories, he might never leave me.

"Now that I think about it, Paul is the first man in my life who doesn't work in some kind of trade. Do bankers dump their women differently than the electricians, laborers, and landscapers of this world?

"Seriously, though," Mary Ann continued, pinching herself, "I've got to stop my mind from concentrating on these silly thoughts. Paul won't disappear. This rambling is just me, Mary Ann, going through one of my insecure moods again. Paul's a solid person. We're in love. We have a future together. We're family. God bless him."

⟡

With only four days left before their scheduled weekend together in Atlanta, Joe called Melissa with bad news.

Just after seven-thirty in the morning, while Melissa was feeling absolutely void of glamour—her body covered by an ancient robe, her face makeup-free, and her hair in need of an overhaul—she listened on the phone to Joe's lament.

"I'm stuck, pure and simple. There's no way I can get out of working on Saturday and Sunday.

"One of the guys in our department just up and quit the other day, without giving any notice. He threw away nine years of seniority as a policeman to take a job driving a truck. For turning in his badge, he'll be taking home a hundred bucks more every week, so I guess none of us here can blame him for making the move."

"Can't someone else besides you fill in for him?" Melissa asked. "How about trying to get a policeman from another town?"

"I've already looked at those options," Joe responded. "For the last few days I've made one frustrating phone call after another trying to line up a replacement—with no luck.

"I'm sorry, Melissa."

Melissa was speechless.

For a time that seemed longer, no doubt, than it really was, she had no idea of what to say.

She pulled the phone away from her ear and stared blankly into the speaker end, as if the phone were at fault. Meanwhile, the fractured thoughts in her mind were racing and stumbling as she attempted, frantically, to put the right words on her lips.

"Are you still there, Melissa?

"Listen, Melissa, I know you must be disappointed," Joe continued. "But at this point there's really nothing else I can do.

"Why don't we try to look on the positive side. Instead of feeling sorry for what could have been, we can make plans to get together on the weekend of Washington's Birthday."

"You mean President's Day?" Melissa whispered, trying to conceal any vocal evidence of the large, wet tears that were now coursing down her cheeks. "That's more than a month from now!"

"According to my new schedule, it's really the only time I can get free, Melissa. I'm going to need some time to break in the rookie that the county promised to send me next week."

"I'm sorry, Joe. I must sound like a real bitch," Melissa answered. "It's just that I was looking forward so very much to our Atlanta weekend."

"I know, Mel. I was, too. Just remember that I love you, Melissa. And I miss you."

"I miss you terribly, Joe. I guess I shouldn't be so selfish. I should show more concern for the things that matter to you—for your life as well as mine. Have you ever had any response yet to those resumes you've been sending out—to the police departments in Pennsylvania and New Jersey?"

"I have, Melissa, but they've all been rejections. The kindest answers I've gotten so far were 'we'll keep your resume on file in case we have an opening.' I'm not discouraged, though. I know it'll take time. Finding a new job is not the easiest thing in the world. But all I have to do is find just one. And once I get that one, then all of the other police departments that rejected me won't matter at all."

"It makes me feel good that you're so confident," Melissa bubbled, her tears almost dry now. "I'm pulling hard for you, Joe. Something will come up, and soon. I just know it."

"I'll call you again next week, Melissa. Love you. Put a big smile on your face for me. It's easier for me, emotionally, to bear being without you when I think of your smile."

"Oh, Joe. I love you, too, and I'm smiling as hard as I can."

Almost as soon as she put down the phone, Melissa once again started to cry. She wished at first she could have Joe's sympathetic shoulder to lean on. But, she realized, if he were here with her, there would be no reason to cry.

"Being so far away from someone you love is unbearable," Melissa told herself. "With Joe being in Florida, it's just the same as if he were thousands of miles away fighting a war in some foreign country—with me sitting home watching the kids. I feel so helpless. And since I'm home without any kids, that's probably also a disadvantage.

"A woman blessed with two little children by her side has two more reasons why her husband would want to come home right away. Or at least she wouldn't have time to worry about her husband being gone."

Her mind continued to wander.

"It reminds me of when I was still a toddler myself and one of my cats was about to give birth. Someone would always be there to ask the inevitable question: 'Are you going to give away the mother and keep one of the kittens?' Did Joe Carlton already decide to give me away, because he has found someone younger?"

All sorts of doubts crossed Melissa's mind. And although she loved Joe and, above all, trusted him, she couldn't help but think that this first broken date—the proposed weekend in Atlanta—was but a harbinger of yet more problems to come in the immediate future.

Logically, Melissa examined her options.

For one, she could take some time off from work right away and speed down to Florida to be with Joe. The benefit of this action would be that she could see him, touch him, and talk to him—satisfying all the needs to have him by her side.

But, although his presence was something she yearned for overwhelmingly, she also considered that at this particular moment, it might be best to play the waiting game.

"Sometimes, the character building that comes from a major disappointment is good for the soul," she rationalized.

"Besides, if I run to him now, it may set a pattern that would result, eventually, in my leaving Philadelphia for good to relocate in Florida.

"And although Islamorada may be a very nice place to visit, as regards job prospects for an upwardly mobile librarian, there would be none there.

"No," she told herself, "what I need during this immediate crisis is female companionship—and advice from someone who has traveled this road before. Also, a double dose of something alcoholic wouldn't hurt, either."

❧

"Am I doomed to remain single?" Melissa asked, while holding onto her fourth margarita of a soul-searching but so far uneventful evening in the cocktail lounge of the Carafe Café.

Jackie Barr, an ever-sympathetic high school chum who had been twice married and twice divorced, was slow to answer.

"I'm not sure," Jackie nodded, while sipping on her own serving of the greenish-tinted tequila. She paused then, contemplatively, to run her finger through the salted edge of the glass, scattering the silence.

"For your sake, Melissa, I hope you're not worried about staying unattached for the rest of your life. Or maybe you're worried about winding up like me?" Jackie grumbled, forcing a laugh. "I may be forty-two years old, but, even at my age, I've still got all of a younger woman's hopes and all of the dreams."

"No," Melissa answered. "It's not exactly the fear of being lonely that bothers me. It's more the worry that Joe may be drifting away from me. If he says, 'Sayonara, Mel,' then I'll start thinking about the other guys who come along later, who'll probably do likewise.

"If Joe leaves, it might be indicative of a pattern that I'm stuck with because of what I am. Melissa the librarian is no longer a single, young virgin who could qualify for the Miss America pageant. My youth is behind me. And rejection may be the penalty for age.

"When I got married to Brady, I was gorgeous. Men would go out of their way to talk to me. When Brady and I were playing golf, for example, any guy who made an errant shot from a nearby fairway would run over and apologize for hitting the ball close to me. Now that I'm older, men don't do things like that anymore. Guys will usually make small talk only to the young, the thin, and the beautiful.

"And what about you, Jackie? After awhile, don't you get tired of putting your heart on the line—to have it knocked down like some pockmarked target in a shooting gallery?"

"One of the things I've learned," Jackie counseled, "is not to let myself think so much about the forest but to concentrate on my own special tree. The same goes for you.

"You've got to forget about everything else—your future, your age, your job—and just worry about keeping your man. Put all of your energies into Joe and hope that, in the meantime, everything else in your life can take care of itself."

"So, if what you say is true, Jackie—my genius, my guru—what's the number one step?"

"The first thing I'd do is to make him jealous. From all we've talked about tonight, this would be your best alternative, believe me. I mean, after all, he is engaged to you. Therefore, he should become jealous if he thinks there's another man trying to get into your pants."

"Won't that be kind of hard to do, what with him living over a thousand miles away?"

"It can be done, Melissa. I read in *Flirt Magazine* not too long ago about a woman who set up a fake recording on the tape that answers her phone calls."

"I guess," Melissa shrugged, cynically, "it wouldn't do any good for me to tell you to stop your story right there, before it begins to sound like one of those farfetched tales that gets passed around at a hairdressing salon on Saturday mornings."

"Now don't be so negative, Melissa. It appears to be something that could really work," Jackie continued, moving to the edge of her seat to begin what was seemingly a straight-faced explanation.

"The way it happened in the magazine story," Jackie went on, "was that this woman wanted to make her guy jealous, so she got her brother to phone her apartment and leave a message on the answering machine—saying that he definitely would show up for their 'date.'"

"But, of course, her brother didn't say he was her brother."

"Of course."

"She rigged the tape so that when her real boyfriend called, he would first hear her standard 'I'm not here now' speech, but then, instead of a beep, the machine would play back part of the tape that had her brother pretending to be the unknown boyfriend—who was going to meet her for champagne, quiche, and a spinach salad at some trendy restaurant."

"Sounds like *Flirt Magazine*, all right."

"But it worked, Melissa. Her real boyfriend got so jealous that he grabbed the next plane available, scooped her up, and whisked her right off to see a Justice of the Peace."

"I think I'll pass on that idea, Jackie. I think I've had enough of these margaritas, too," Melissa concluded, rising shakily to leave. The implausibility of Jackie's suggestions signaled to her that the evening's jabber would no longer be productive—that, coupled with her increasing inability to keep from slurring her words.

"When I wake up with a hangover tomorrow morning," Melissa added, "I may change my mind. But for now, I have to give Joe the benefit of the doubt. In my current situation, that translates into a do-nothing decision.

"Up to this point, Joe has done everything honest and up-front in our relationship. So, if I were to make a rash move now that shows I distrust him, or indicates that I'm some sort of a conniving broad, then it would be me, Melissa the Terrible, who wouldn't be worthy of Joe 'White Knight' Carlton."

Chapter 10

Mary Ann experienced a great deal of happiness during the time period immediately following her engagement. For one thing, Paul seemed to spend much more time with her and the girls. He would visit almost every evening—a ritual that helped him learn the role of being a father. He assisted the girls with their homework, gave them advice whenever they asked for it, and even used his skill with a pair of scissors to trim their curls and bangs.

"Melissa is the only one who won't let me cut her hair," Paul told Mary Ann.

"That's all right," Mary Ann countered, consoling him. "I guess only her Mom is allowed to see her if she bleeds—not her stepfather-to-be."

For Valentine's Day, Paul gave Mary Ann yet another gift of jewelry—a pearl necklace. Its beauty added a luxurious touch to her clothing whenever she and Paul would go out to dinner or to a show.

"They're freshwater pearls," Mary Ann explained, showing them to her daughters. "That's why they look like Rice Krispies."

Mary Ann believed that her ever-glistening engagement ring was having a stoplight effect on unwanted suitors.

"At work, plenty of men, especially the guys in the plant, used to say hello to me," Mary Ann recalled. "And when I'd be shopping for food or just walking around town, other men would occasionally try to strike up conversations.

"Not anymore. This big engagement ring probably scares them off. I'd always get annoyed when those guys with the dirty elbows and the bad breath would try to be friendly. The words they never said were spoken by their appearance and their facial expressions—dirt, lust, and dirty minds.

"It makes me happy that I don't have to worry about guys coming on to me much anymore."

Mary Ann's tranquil existence, however, was disturbed one Friday afternoon in March when she was laid off from her full-time job at the power plant. Paul picked her up after work and was the first to hear the bad news.

"They say they don't have enough work anymore for three secretaries," she explained, trying to hold back her tears. "But I think they got rid of me because I'm always speaking my mind. Boss or no boss, I always let people know how I feel.

"I guess," she added, reflectively, "that I'd be hell on the Senate floor—because I'm a good complainer. But it's probably best I'm not in politics. Without a doubt, I'm one of those who would definitely get shot.

"I won't miss the place, I'll just miss working with the few good friends I made there. The long hours, the drafty building, and the low pay made it a not-so-pleasant place to work. Yet, my friends will always be my friends, and I'll get together with them whenever I can.

"Do you realize," Mary Ann asked Paul, changing the subject slightly, "that most of the waitresses in Pottstown get a salary of only one or two dollars an hour? They have to depend on tips. That's not fair at all."

Mary Ann's tears were visible now, but she seemed determined not to let the layoff get the best of her. Paul was amazed at how Mary Ann, in the midst of a major lifetime disappointment, was able to look out the car window and point to a small storefront only a block or so from her apartment.

"That yarn store over there," she noted. "That's where I'm going to enroll in a class to learn how to do counted cross-stitch."

"Whether you're working at a job," Paul added, "or you're doing this cross-stitch, I'll be around to help you. Don't worry about the bills. I'll pay them. Your role right now is to relax for a while and then look for work. Maybe that convenience store will be able to give you some part-time work again. But whatever you do, don't take something 'just because it's a job.' Keep looking. Stick it out until you find what you really like. We can afford to wait."

"I remember the last time I lost a job," Mary Ann continued, with quivers of a smile slowly replacing her tears. "Back then, whenever I'd cash my unemployment check and go to the supermarket, I'd wind up spending more than half of the money I had in the world on a week's worth of food. We were poor then, too, and we had bad water in our apartment.

"So I had to borrow water from a neighbor for me and the girls. When you're working long hours and you're forced to carry heavy buckets of borrowed water, then that's when you worry about whether you're still sane and whether the world around you is still sane."

"Forget all about the water," Paul responded, in a positive tone. "As long as I can stay healthy, I'll do my best to keep all of us in champagne."

∽

Melissa had every item in her house arranged and spruced perfectly for Joe's visit.

For several days prior to President's Day weekend, she attacked every chore—from cleaning the rooms to stocking up on all of Joe's favorite foods.

Her house was spotless. In the bedroom, she had installed new curtains and matching pillowcases. The yellow on blue pastel designs, she thought, now gave the room an airy, warm, Florida look.

For the three nights of Joe's proposed stay, she had purchased sufficient gourmet edibles that the two of them would never have to leave the house for dinner.

Her food-shopping spree included the purchase of gigantic sirloin steaks, a huge bag of frozen shrimp, and two cans of expensive backfin crabmeat. A third can she'd bought the week before provided a practice run when she had satisfactorily cooked a crab au gratin recipe—Joe's favorite entrée. Coke had purred continuously throughout his pussycat sampling.

New clothing was another result of Melissa's recent shopping. In addition to designer jeans, a pink sundress, and two new nighties—one in basic black and another in yellow—Melissa also picked up some men's underwear for Joe at a center city department store.

She giggled after walking away from the sales counter, tucking into her bag a sexy, matched shirt-and-shorts ensemble in see-through mesh. The flesh-toned hue was certain to complement Joe's suntan.

On Thursday, the day before Joe's arrival, Melissa indulged herself in a haircut, facial, and new makeup treatment at Jeffrey's Rittenhouse Square Beauty Salon.

"It seems to pick up my confidence whenever I get my hair done," she told herself. "To me, a cut-wash-and-blow-dry is like a dose of the best vitamin supplements that money can buy. I don't know why, but I feel better, and I can even think more clearly after a visit to Jeffrey's."

Melissa had considered, seriously, being completely nude when she opened her front door to greet Joe. After some thought, though, she decided against it, opting instead for wearing the new pink dress.

"But I won't have any underwear on," she smirked, privately. "Plus, for a sexy touch, I'll paint my toenails hot pink and go barefoot."

&

At about eight-thirty Friday night, Melissa peeked out through the living room curtains to see an airport limousine stop in the middle of her street, right on schedule.

She watched, crouched in hiding, as Joe paid the fare and then turned slowly to walk toward the house. Without waiting, Melissa opened the door and stood, smiling broadly, until he walked up the steps and put his arms around her. After several brief kisses, he picked up his suitcase and followed Melissa into the living room.

When they were both inside the house, they embraced again, alternately kissing on the lips and cheeks and finally holding hands while staring closely into each other's eyes.

Melissa assumed that Joe's next move would be directed toward her sundress. She expected him to undo the buttons in the back and slide the top part of it down through her arms and hands, letting it drop past her hips and onto the floor. But, instead of beginning such a bawdy attack on her body, he stepped back—and then he posed a question.

"How about a cup of coffee for a weary traveler?"

So, while Melissa puttered in the kitchen with cups and boiling water, Joe led the conversation with small talk about hot and sunny Islamorada weather, cold and damp Philadelphia weather, and the bumper-to-bumper non-Florida traffic he'd encountered during his ride to her house from Philadelphia International Airport.

Finally, when they were seated across from each other in the breakfast nook of Melissa's small kitchen, Joe looked at her directly, eye-to-eye, and began to speak.

"Melissa, for weeks now I've been looking forward to this visit. I've daydreamed after coming through that front door of yours, lifting you into my arms, and carrying you up to your bedroom."

Melissa smiled, sheepishly, because she, too, had shared that daydream. But, as she gazed quickly, back and forth, between Joe and her coffee cup, she decided not to interrupt, waiting instead for him to continue.

"I guess I could have stalled before starting this conversation—like waiting until after we had sex," he commented, almost in a whisper. "Maybe I should have held off until we got our fill of each other's bodies. But I have this burning feeling inside of me that says I have to tell you right away."

"What it comes down to," Joe stuttered, "is . . . is that I'm having second thoughts about us getting married."

By his hesitation, it was obvious to Melissa that Joe was experiencing difficulty in delivering this blockbuster of a message. Yet, he went on.

"And I want to share these second thoughts with you, Melissa, so that you can tell me either that I'm crazy, or that I should take the next plane back to Islamorada."

"Come on, Joe, just tell me what your problems are," Melissa answered, quickly, almost begging.

Then, sensing his disintegrating composure—how he was struggling with his words and fighting to keep his head upright—she reached over and clasped both his hands inside hers. Like a mother might say to a child, she implored of him, "Tell me, Joe, get it all out. I have a right to know."

"To be perfectly honest, Melissa, things haven't been going too well for me. And I'm not a very happy person."

"What exactly do you mean?"

"Lately, I feel as though my life has been turned inside-out and upside-down, what with the upcoming wedding and that elusive job I haven't been able to find. Maybe I'm getting too old for all of this upheaval, this sudden change."

"Are you saying, then, that your unhappiness is my fault?"

"Fault's not the right word, Melissa. I love you—just the way you are.

But I've been thinking that maybe I was never meant to be a married man."

Although by this point in the conversation Melissa had caught the drift of what Joe was trying to say, and though he had said it all so gently, she was still wide-eyed and open-mouthed at the bottom-line meaning of his comments.

"I guess I've come to realize, Melissa, that I've turned the corner in my life. With all of the rejections I've gotten on those resumes I've sent out, I can no longer consider myself a young man who has promise. And since this potential for future success doesn't seem to exist anymore, I feel like I've been severed from all of my dreams—and I guess, subconsciously, I'm blaming you, even though it's not your fault that I feel this way."

"So, if it's not my fault, Joe, then why are you trying to cut me off from the rest of your life, if that's what you're really trying to say?"

"You don't want to spend the next thirty or forty years living with a failure, and that's what I am—one absolute, no questions about it, royal failure."

"First of all, you're not a failure," Melissa insisted, her understanding manner now shifting toward anger. "Just because you haven't gotten a job yet shouldn't have anything to do with whether we love one another. And how do you get off telling me that I wouldn't want to spend the rest of my life with you? I've already made that decision. I do want to spend the rest of my life with you. I do. I really do."

"Look, Melissa, the job I haven't been able to find is not just a job. It would be a major career move. And despite all my years of police experience, I've gotten a big zero of a response. The reason for this, without a doubt, is because of my age. Simply put, I'm just too old. All of the police departments today want younger men. This is definitely a disturbing situation. It's not just something that we can ignore by sticking our heads in the sand. Instead, it's what both you and I have to recognize as a significant, insurmountable problem. And, significant problems don't go away with time.

"Tell me, Melissa, have you considered what we might do if I can't get a job near Philly? If that happens, would you want me to move up here anyway? Would you want me to be a bum while you go to work every day?"

Hesitating for just a few seconds, Melissa then admitted, reluctantly, that she had never even given thought to the "Joe Gets No Job" scenario.

"I still believe, deep down in my heart, that you'll find a job. And yes, you can move up here anyway. I can support you until you find work. Maybe that would be better anyway. If you're living here, it will be easier for you to apply for work in this part of the country, a lot easier."

"That is, truly, quite generous of you, Melissa, but I think you're missing the point. You're forgetting how uncomfortable I would feel if I had to live here while you pay all the bills. In that kind of situation, with you as the breadwinner, I just wouldn't be the same Joe Carlton."

"So what you're saying then is that your career as a policeman is more important than me. It's either that, or you're trying to weasel out of marring a divorcee. I guess I'm just second-hand goods.

"You prefer the joys of being a traveling playboy, don't you, stopping by, digging in, and then moving on again? Just tell me, honestly, Joe, are you trying to find an excuse for walking out of my life?"

"Now, try to calm down a little, Melissa. I know this is very serious stuff here, but really I don't think I'm looking for an excuse. It's just that I can't see both of us being happy if I'm sponging off you while you take care of all the expenses. And please, Melissa, the fact that you've been divorced is immaterial. That has nothing to do with it at all."

"You're a man, so you must have considered it," Melissa intoned, small tears now appearing at the edges of her eyes. "If I were single, even if I had had a dozen affairs, single would be easier for a man to take, wouldn't it? To a man, getting married and limiting himself to one woman is enough of an ego shock. But if a man is getting himself married to a divorced woman, it's even worse. It's like buying a used car. Your male ego can't stand being second in line, can it? This is your real insurmountable problem, isn't it, Joe? Because ever since you were a little boy, you've been pampered into thinking you're special, and no one who's special likes to take second-hand goods."

By now, Melissa's tears were flowing steadily on her cheeks and down onto her chin. With her elbows on the table now, she had her head lowered. She used the napkin she had set for her coffee to dry the water on her face and eyes. When she had finished, the crumpled napkin had a distinctive smell, like the sudden opening of a makeup case.

"Melissa, I don't know how else to say this, but you are not second-hand goods. You are lovely, you are precious to me, and I care for you so very much. I just ask that we postpone making any more plans until I've had time to think about my life and where I'm headed in this world. I'm not going to abandon you, Melissa. I just wanted to talk to you and tell you, as frankly as possible, how I really feel."

Joe was standing now, right alongside a seated Melissa.

And though he may have appeared twice as tall as she, it was he who seemed vulnerable. By holding out his handkerchief like a defeated general waving a white flag, he tried to win her trust.

Melissa, turning her head ever so slightly toward Joe's gaze, flashed the tiniest of smiles as she grasped the handkerchief.

With what seemed like a reactive motion, Joe placed his hand on Melissa's shoulder as she dabbed at the remainder of her tears.

"Come, Melissa. Let's go into the living room and sit on the sofa. I think we both need to relax."

Within a few seconds, Joe was holding her tightly as they reclined on the sofa. The only light now shining came at an around-the-corner angle from the kitchen they had just left.

Then, for about half an hour, even though arm-in-arm, they said nothing to one another.

Melissa, with her legs now stretched outward on the sofa space to her left, immersed herself in cold, survival-like thoughts while Joe clutched her close to him.

As she lay resting, listening to the nearby grandfather clock tick away the minutes, Melissa realized she hadn't said a word since her outburst about second-hand goods. And although she was experiencing a slight bit of guilt for having accused Joe of not valuing their relationship, the volleys she'd fired had left her feeling successfully purged of most of the fears she'd been harboring.

She really didn't know what she wanted to say next. So, while she remained cuddled next to Joe, staring across the darkness of the living room, she forced herself to think logic instead of fury.

Hoping she was being realistic, she attempted, in her mind, to give Joe the benefit of the doubt, trying to ferret out the hidden plusses in his sudden resolve that "we postpone making any more plans."

"It's true," she told herself, "that if he has been running around with some Florida floozy, he wouldn't have had to give me his little speech at all. He could be shacking up with a woman like that every night of the week in Islamorada, and I'd never know anything about it.

"Also," she realized, "Joe does deserve some credit for being an honest and up-front person. As soon as he walked through the door, he could have had all the sex he wanted and then dropped his bombshell. Instead, he got right to the point. I would be feeling a lot worse right now if he had had his fill of my body BEFORE he started talking.

"Of course," Melissa continued, searching deeper for a reason, "perhaps all he wants is to have me available for steady sex—with no commitment on his part. I have to think of that possibility as his primary goal. Joe has been free of commitments for so long now that he probably thinks our charted relationship, with day-by-day plans that lead toward marriage, has sort of put him behind bars."

Without realizing it, Melissa began talking aloud to herself.

"When I was a little girl, my stepfather took me deep-sea fishing in Ocean City," she said. "He told me that when I hooked a fish, I shouldn't pull hard right away, because the line might snap. I should let the fish swim away a bit with the line until he gets tired. Only then should I pull him in."

Melissa suddenly sensed a silence, thinking that Joe might have dozed off while holding her in his arms. So, without any accompanying body motion, she started whispering his name.

"Joe . . . Joe . . . are you awake?"

"Mmmm, yes," he answered, obviously groggy but moving toward consciousness after a brief snooze.

"I went fishing once in Ocean City," he mumbled, while clearing his head, "off the 55th Street bridge. Uncle Steve took me."

"Should I keep the ring?"

"What?"

"Joe, should I keep it, the engagement ring?"

"Absolutely, Mel. 'Til death do us part."

Outwardly, Melissa presented a cheerful appearance through the remainder of President's Day weekend. But despite her smile and the warm feelings she experienced whenever Joe clutched her hand or held her body close to his, the magical moments could not be duplicated. Unforgettable memories were not in the making.

Physically, Melissa felt as though she had fallen victim to a constant, dulling toothache. Emotionally, however, it was her heart that had suffered a setback.

Melissa and Joe made love twice that weekend—on Saturday afternoon and again on Sunday night. Happily, the erotic pleasure still existed for both of them.

Joe seemed thoroughly exhausted at the end of each of these sessions, just as he had earlier in their relationship. Once again his body had been spent, literally, in two highly successful physical efforts that pleased both Melissa and him.

And while she was making love to Joe, Melissa managed to forget completely about the new uncertainties of their immediate future. Pressing her naked body next to his and experiencing his strong, powerful technique left her as satisfied as ever.

Both of these bedroom encounters left Melissa with a warm glow that lasted long after Joe had recovered from his exhaustion. But part of what she felt was a hit-and-miss, fleeting pang of guilt soon after the conclusion of their sex. For though she had knowingly curtailed her foreplay, Joe himself showed no restraint, giving to her every delicious portion of all that she had been accustomed to receiving.

For the remainder of the time they spent together that weekend, Melissa and Joe joked with each other, watched a R-rated movie on cable television, and, in general, enjoyed the couples-only solitude of an extended domestic holiday.

Melissa was successful in preparing the dinners that she had planned in advance of his arrival. To Joe's credit, he assisted—by grating some Parmesan cheese for the crab au gratin and by cutting mushrooms and onions for their bounteous salads.

The only time they ventured out of Melissa's house was to take a long

Sunday afternoon bus ride to the Philadelphia Art Museum. In the uncrowded confines of this majestic building, overlooking the Schuylkill River, they gazed at the works of the old masters and were treated to a special exhibit highlighting artifacts recovered from early "Pennsylvania Dutch" settlements.

Even some of the largest rooms in the museum were empty of visitors. In two such spacious areas, Melissa and Joe exchanged impromptu hugs and innocent, cheek-to-cheek kisses—just like a pair of preteens who weren't sure exactly what they were doing but knew that it was fun.

As they exited the museum, Joe stood at the top of the outdoor steps, flexing his muscles à la that fictional film star, Rocky Balboa.

"You're mugging, and there's no camera," Melissa commented, wryly. "Save it for the evening news."

"TV news don't mean nothing to me, Adrian," Joe answered, mimicking Rocky's punch-drunk drawl, "unless you'se the one who's watching."

⸎

Finally, when it came time for Monday afternoon and Joe's departure, Melissa, as usual, wished that she could be in his company for just a little while longer.

The pain of being rejected, however, still smarted within her. Perhaps that's why she didn't offer to drive him to the airport and, instead, called a cab.

"Better he should leave the same way he got here," Melissa reasoned. "Since I have this hunch that I may never see him again, I don't want to have to remember the foolishness of chasing him to the airport. It's bad enough that I'll be haunted by the memory of how he arrived here last Friday, smiling and suntanned, and the realistic hopes I had when I watched him stride toward the house. For my sake, I hope I don't cry, and I hope I don't wish to go back in time whenever I look out into the street and see nothing, no one. The image I keep of his presence as he walked up my front steps will be balanced by the remembrance that I sent him packing."

In their farewells, Melissa and Joe formulated no plans to see each other again on any definite future date.

"I'll call you in a few days," was all Joe could offer. "And I'll keep sending out my resumes. Who knows? We might get lucky!"

When the cab arrived, idling noisily at the curb, Melissa followed Joe only with her eyes as he ambled through the cold and pulled open the rear door on the passenger's side. The wind was at his back now as he looked up to throw her one final kiss.

Melissa responded by thrusting out her left hand to acknowledge his retreating salute, keeping the right one tucked tightly behind her—fingers crossed. And from his seat in the cab, Joe flashed that patented, shutter-like sparkle of a smile. Then, with one last wistful wave of his arm, he was gone.

As the cab approached the corner, Melissa couldn't stand her restraint any longer. She dashed from the house frantically waving at the cab, but Joe never turned around. She stood there shivering in her jeans and sweatshirt as a light snow fell around her. The snowflakes mingled with the tears now coursing freely down her cheeks.

Chapter 11

Unemployment was always on her mind. And although Mary Ann tried to busy herself with activity-type distractions, she couldn't help thinking about her current status as a woman who was no longer a permanent member of the work force.

"Unlike in the past, when several eviction notices were tacked on my front door," Mary Ann realized, "Paul's financial help now has made it easier for me to adjust to being jobless. I realize that being out of work creates a certain state of mind, as well, aside from the money problems. Unemployment can be depressing, and I'm grateful for Paul's emotional support. The last time I lost a job and couldn't find new work, the kids helped me crumple up all of our overdue bills. Then we started a little fire on the sidewalk. That tiny protest had no impact on anyone else, but it was good for our souls."

The more Mary Ann thought about her most recent layoff, the more she was convinced that her bosses got rid of her because of Paul.

"They figured I didn't need the money as much as the other two girls I worked with, plain and simple," she concluded. "The bosses know that Paul makes more than enough to support me."

During the time that she continued to search for work, Mary Ann also kept busy with her needlepoint class (every Thursday night), her sign language studies (Tuesdays), and her singing lessons (Saturday mornings). She also carried one of Paul's watercolor paintings to a shop over at the mall and picked out a frame and matting for it.

"I never really wanted a college education, but there are some things I've always been interested in—singing, signing, and anything artsy-craftsy. If I find out I like these things even more, then great. If I find out that they bore me after a while, then at least I've tried, and I won't be going to my grave wondering what they would have been like. Some day in the future I might be using sign language to help deaf kids. Or, I might be singing Christmas carols while being backed up by a live orchestra. If I keep up my studies, who knows? I might reach goals I haven't even dreamed of yet."

Mary Ann was aware that her current craving for self-enrichment courses, although not overly expensive, was costing Paul a fair amount of money. So, in a cost-cutting move, she canceled her and Paul's favorite pastimes: gourmet dinners in restaurants and shopping just for the sake of shopping. She even eliminated another cherished diversion—their racetrack jaunts.

"I'm a cheap date now," she declared, convincing Paul that their entertainment should be confined to free museums, long walks, and family-type restaurants.

Paul was happy to oblige, and, overall, he seemed to enjoy their continuing status as an engaged couple.

Mary Ann did notice, however, that Paul's interest in sex seemed to have diminished recently. Immediately, she began to think that she might be at fault.

"Aside from my real sinus headaches, which stopped us twice," she recalled, "I am definitely to blame for two other fake headaches that hit me when I just wasn't in the mood."

After their sexual fasting had passed the 30-day mark, Mary Ann did a bit of soul searching.

"This may just be some sort of a power struggle," she told herself. "Ever since I've been out of work, he's been controlling my life even more than before. I depend on him for everything now. Maybe I'm rebelling because of this control.

"I've gained some weight lately, too. I guess about ten pounds. I can't feel good about that. But maybe my coolness toward sex just turned downright cold because of Paul's lack of interest. The more I think about this, the more it sounds like the chicken and the egg."

Mary Ann and Paul even had their first real argument. Previously, whenever they'd gone to the movies by themselves, without the girls, they'd pick pictures that Mary Ann liked—action adventure or slapstick comedy. Paul now stated that he was tired of those kinds of movies and said he wanted to see some "think pieces."

"We've been together for over a year now," Mary Ann reflected. "We should be able to sit down and talk this out.

"What we'll do is go to that same Chinese restaurant we visited a few months ago where I first tasted leechee nuts. We talked for the longest time about whether the leechee nuts tasted more like pears or more like mandarin oranges.

"After dessert that night, it was quiet and we talked, and talked, and talked.

"I hope Paul's ready for a long conversation.

"I am."

&

Dutifully, like a husband who might have been away on an extended sales trip, Joe called Melissa at about eight o'clock in the evening on Tuesdays and Fridays.

And like the wife who is ever faithful, Melissa stayed at home to receive each of these calls.

"I guess he feels he owes it to me," she reflected, sadly. "But it's really an insult. The phone calls could be his way of keeping me on a string. If he ever decides he wants physical contact again instead of just hearing my voice, he can claim that we've never really lost touch with one another."

In their conversations, Melissa and Joe talked about the tourists who were crowding the Florida Keys, the blizzard that was immobilizing Philadelphia for an entire weekend, the police departments that were rejecting Joe's job applications, and the occasional workaday smiles that were highlighting Melissa's Monday-to-Friday routines as a reference librarian.

Like old times, they laughed together when she told the story of the patron who was astounded when informed that Philadelphia's phone book information pages were printed only in English and not in Italian.

And, as always, Melissa and Joe prefaced every good-bye with a vague promise to get together as soon as possible.

One Friday night in late March, after she had finished her chat with Joe, Melissa returned almost mechanically to the mindless chore of removing the dry dishes from the dishwasher, one-by-one, and putting them in their resting places in the overhead cabinets.

Suddenly, within only a few minutes from the time she had hung up the phone, Melissa heard it ring once more.

Thinking it was Joe again, who might wish to impart some sort of an afterthought to their conversation, Melissa casually lifted the receiver.

"Hello."

"Melissa? How are you doing, my dear? This is Joe's Uncle Steve."

"Oh. Hi, Uncle Steve. Sorry if I sounded listless, but you surprised me."

"I'm usually full of surprises."

"I just got finished talking with Joe, and I thought it must be him calling me back. How have you been?"

"Fine, just fine, Melissa. No real big problems, just little ones. Listen, the reason I called was to ask you if you'd like to come on over to Jersey and spend some time cheering up an old man. Like lunch maybe tomorrow or Sunday. I'll do all the cooking."

"Well, I'm flattered, Uncle Steve. I really am. And I don't even have to look at my appointment calendar. I know that tomorrow would be good for me. What time?"

"What about high noon?"

"Sounds great. Should I bring some white wine, or a bottle of red?"

"Just yourself."

&

Melissa wasn't quite sure why she had agreed so quickly to have lunch with Joe's Uncle Steve. True, she really did like the old gentleman, but considering the current deterioration of her now bleak relationship with Joe, she was a bit surprised that he would ask her at all.

Certainly, Uncle Steve must know that she and Joe haven't exactly been seeing each other on a nightly basis.

The determining factor, though, was that Melissa was too kind a person to turn down an invite from Uncle Steve. Besides, she did enjoy his company.

Also, Melissa's constantly calculating mind perked up at the possibility that she could make some points with Joe through his uncle.

During her traffic-free drive to New Jersey, Melissa wondered if she would be seeing Uncle Steve for the last time. Her reasoning had nothing to do with the condition of Uncle Steve's health, but rather with the likelihood that she and Joe were probably headed, without too much doubt, toward an "official" breakup.

Melissa knew from her own cold personal experiences that the relatives and friends of one's lover seem to disappear into oblivion when the lover finally says good-bye. And with Uncle Steve seeming to be such a genuinely warm and pleasant human being, the loss of his friendship would be like giving up a cream-topped dessert in addition to the main course.

Weather-wise, compared to her first visit with Uncle Steve during the cold and wet snowstorm of Christmas Eve, today's driving conditions were much more tolerable. Countless rays of sunlight beamed through a cloudless sky, and the late March air was following the dictates of the calendar.

At shortly before the noon hour, the heavens' clear, cerulean glow was dominant in all noticeable directions. And with a temperature already exceeding sixty degrees, it was a fit beginning for the twentieth of March. More importantly, it felt like spring.

Melissa was glad she had chosen to wear bright, cheerful colors. Her blue and white dress was complemented by an airy, lace-like sweater and blue, summery shoes.

While she was thinking about her clothes, Melissa remembered the array of watercolors bedecking the walls throughout Uncle Steve's house. Most were horseracing scenes, with jockeys in bright pastels riding roan and chestnut thoroughbreds.

Melissa also recalled a light-hearted comment Uncle Steve had made about Sally, his late wife. "She was taller than me," Uncle Steve had said, "so tall that she could have been a bouncer in a jockeys' bar."

As she began her approach to his house, Melissa saw that there would be no need to knock on Uncle Steve's front door. For long before she pulled her car into his driveway, she could see him waving hello from the porch.

Uncle Steve was dressed in a racy pair of electric-green golf duffer's slacks and a two-tone, green and yellow, striped shirt. When he offered his hand to help Melissa exit from her car, he flashed a foot-long smile that would have melted a golf hustler's heart.

"Old Man Winter has finally hit the road," he chuckled, in his normally loud conversational tone. "And old man Steve enjoys talking to young women who dress correctly for the warmer months. In January and February, unfortunately, too many layers of bulky clothing just kill the art of girl watching."

In a sheepish manner, typical of her introverted nature, Melissa looked immediately to her hemline. Then, as soon as she had completed this modesty reaction, she remembered Uncle Steve's penchant for flattery. It was a style of chatter no longer fashionable, but charming nonetheless. A much younger man with the same line of compliments could be branded a chauvinist.

Melissa also recalled, warmly, that older men like Uncle Steve have the ability to make her feel younger and sexier much more so than men her own age. Maybe that's why so many women fall for older men. The same feeling works on men, too. Just as the guy in his thirties can be smitten by a teenage girl's youthful sex appeal, so can an elderly gent start to swoon over a woman who's reached her so-called prime.

When they entered his house, Uncle Steve continued voicing his phrases of praise, telling Melissa that her "dainty" sweater and "colorful" dress accentuated a "trim and alluring figure."

"You look like some of those beautiful girl jockeys that are riding thoroughbred racehorses these days," Uncle Steve pointed out. "Not only are they pretty but some of them are much better than the boys at handling horses."

The food in Uncle Steve's luncheon spread was pleasant on the eyes as well as the palate. It was a true potpourri of traditional Polish foods. The red beet soup was warm and tangy, providing the perfect beginning for a series of entrées such as meaty kielbasa topped with a sparkling yellow sauerkraut, potato and cheese-filled pierogis that were browned at the edges, and sweet-smelling golabki—ground beef wrapped in whitish cabbage and swimming in a light tomato sauce.

"Ever since Joe told me that you were part-Polish, too, just like us," Uncle Steve grinned, proudly, "I've been waiting for a chance to feed you a spread of my homeland recipes. These are all authentic, from my mother, who was born in Poland. In fact, I have a copy of every one of my Polish recipes. As soon as we're finished with the dessert, I'm going to give them to you to keep. I doubt if anyone has ever written these down before. I think they passed from generation to generation by word of mouth. Naturally, I don't want the recipes to die when I die.

"When Joe told me that you also like to cook, I knew then that you were just the right person to give them to."

The dessert, as Uncle Steve promised, was delectable. Cheese babka, a combination of bread and coffee cake, was satisfying to eat. The krusciki, a kind of flaky, butter crust cookie topped with white-powdered sugar, was what Uncle Steve called a "Polish potato chip."

"Nobody in this world can eat just one krusciki," he beamed, while doing his part to finish a moderate-sized helping.

In deference to the enjoyment of their luncheon, Uncle Steve waited until the meal was complete before mentioning the "problem" with Joe. And it came as no surprise to Melissa that Uncle Steve knew about the separation that Joe had requested.

"Joe's fears about never getting a job in the Philadelphia area are very typical of how he thinks," Uncle Steve announced.

"How is that?"

"Ever since he was a little kid, he's had a tendency not to take any really big chances. Like when he plays the horses, for example. He'll always put his money on the favorites, never betting any long shots.

"What he should do right away is move up to Philly and stay with you. That's what I told him, straight out. I know he can get himself a job eventually."

"That's what I told him, too, Uncle Steve. But I couldn't convince him."

Leaning back in his chair now and looking all the world like a gambler who was about to turn over an ace, Steve lowered the volume of his voice as his counsel continued.

"To be honest, I've been thinking about you two folks for quite awhile now. And as long as you, personally, Melissa, won't consider me an old man who meddles in other people's business, I'd like to give you some advice."

"Oh, I'd love to have your opinion," Melissa answered, as she sipped on her second glass of white wine, at the same time relaxing loosely on an easy chair whose seat was wide enough for three of her. "You're not a meddler at all. Go right ahead, tell me. I'm all ears."

"Why don't you surprise him, Melissa? Get yourself on a plane to Florida without letting Joe know ahead of time. And when you get down there to Islamorada, just tell him that you've come along to help him pack and move up to Philly with you. Believe me, I know the guy. If you're firm, and you're the leader, he'll follow as long as it's something that he wants, too.

"And since I'm positive that he really wants to be with you, I know that this surprise move is the right thing for you to do. Get down there and grab hold of him, Melissa. Just take him and tell him he belongs to you."

Melissa's immediate reaction was silence.

She sat, biting on her bottom lip while staring directly into Uncle Steve's friendly blue eyes. It was as if she were waiting for him to add an oral P.S.—just a few more words that would guarantee the success of his suggestion.

Finally, though, it was Melissa who broke that silence.

"A move like that would take a lot of courage on my part," she spoke, sitting upright now. "And, seriously, I don't really know if I'd be gutsy enough to do such a thing.

"I guess what I fear most about your idea, Uncle Steve, is the real possibility that Joe would give me a flat turndown once I got to Florida. Emotionally, something like that could be crushing."

"He won't turn you down, Melissa. I'm positive of that. I've been a successful gambler all of my life. This would work, definitely.

"Of course, I didn't expect that you'd agree with me one hundred percent. I figured you'd have some reservations about my plan. And, I realize that this is something you'll have to do entirely on your own. The first step for you, unquestionably, is to convince yourself that I'm right."

"Oh, Uncle Steve," Melissa replied, "you must know you're absolutely right so far, at least about my initial reaction."

"Your wariness is justified to some extent, my dear, in that there will always be certain situations in life when you should be careful. These are set-ups that will always do you dirt," Uncle Steve laughed, "like playing cards with a guy named 'Doc' or eating at a restaurant called 'Mom's.'

"My suggestion, however, is the opposite of any of those sucker punches. Putting yourself out on a limb by going to Florida may appear to be crazy, but really, it isn't. My idea is the equivalent of you betting your money on a long shot, because you're one of only a few people with valuable inside information.

"What I'm giving you is a hot tip, Melissa. It's coming from somebody who knows this 'horse' very well. And whether you realize it or not, you're about as close to a no-lose situation as anyone can ever come.

"It's an undisputed fact, Melissa, that Joe has always asked me for advice. And once you assert yourself by going to Florida, I don't expect that situation will change. If he's in any doubt at all about what to do, he's sure to ask me for my opinion once again. It's true, though, that you might sweep him off his feet once you're down there, and the two of you will elope. But if he's hesitant at all, he'll call me, and then I'll tell him he should marry you. So, if I were you, I'd make that trip. Think about my plan, okay?"

"I will.

"Uncle Steve, I have something I need to ask you that's been worrying me lately. Do you think Joe's reluctance to move to this area has anything to do with his feelings for his former fiancée, Becky? I know when he first told me about her he still seemed to be really moved by the experience."

"Well, Melissa. I was around during Joe and Becky's courtship. And I won't lie to you and say that Joe didn't love her. Gosh, it would be hard for anybody not to love Becky. She was so 'motherly' I guess is the word for it. She was always ready to take care of people. I think for Joe, she became the mother he lost as a child.

"Yes, that's a kind of love. But what he feels for you, Melissa, that's something totally different. That's what marriages are made of, what sustains them through the years. You need much more from a wife than

a mother. No, Melissa. You're the one for Joe. And don't give Becky another thought. I know that Joe hasn't, ever since he fell for you.

"And one last thing, if you would," Uncle Steve offered, with a strange,
guru-like grin. "Don't let Joe know that you were here to see me. Is that
a promise?"

"I promise."

Chapter 12

"I've been worrying too much about you, M.A. And because of that worry, I think our relationship has suffered."

With those exact words, Paul began his explanation for the lack of sexual activity.

"I want everything to be perfect for you. You've been denied so much in the past just because you couldn't afford things. Now, my goal is to make sure you never have to worry about money again—for as long as you live.

"I want you to find work again, because I know you're unhappy being unemployed. I see you unhappy, and I get uptight. Then when I'm uptight, I can't relax and be intimate with you. I also get irritable when I'm uptight. And when I'm irritable, it's very easy for me to get into arguments—even over stupid little things like what TV show or what movie we should watch."

"I'm also to blame," Mary Ann noted, contributing an apology of her own to the post-dessert discussion. "Without a job, I feel so much at your mercy. For instance, I have a new car sitting out there in the street, and you're making payments on it. What would happen to that car if you walked out of my life? Not that you *would* walk out on me, but I guess that's how I think when I don't have any steady work to keep my mind busy.

"I admit, Paul, that I've been cold toward you physically. But now that I recognize the problem I'll change. I'm still worried, though, that you might not like me as much since I've gained weight. I've only put on about ten pounds, but it feels like a lot more.

"Maybe I should apply for guard work or some kind of security job," Mary Ann continued, tongue-in-cheek. "With this extra weight, I'll be more effective whenever I have to kick a few rear ends."

"The weight you've put on isn't even noticeable," Paul answered. "You're the type of person who never looks fat. And as for your job-hunting, I'll tell you about a deal I have for you. When you find a job, we'll celebrate by taking a big trip somewhere as soon as we can. The big trip can be our honeymoon. Of course, we might not be able to go until your new bosses let you take a vacation. But I won't mind waiting.

"So, how's that deal sound to you?"

Mary Ann wasted little time before contacting a travel agent. She picked up brochures for trips to Hawaii, Bermuda, Ireland, and several islands off the coast of Florida—four areas she'd always wanted to visit.

"I'm picking places we can't possibly get to by cross-country bus," she reasoned, inwardly.

Back when she was fifteen years old, Mary Ann's mother had put her on a bus from Harrisburg to Chicago. Mary Ann stayed in Illinois with her grandmother for six months until financial problems were settled at home.

"I never hated my mom for putting me on that bus," Mary Ann remembered. "But ever since then, I've never taken a long-distance bus ride. There was a certain finality to being put on that bus to Chicago. I was worried I'd never come home again, even to visit. I don't think I would have felt that way if I'd have been driven to Chicago in a car."

While Mary Ann continued to send for travel literature describing her personally selected faraway places, an occurrence on the home front took on a special meaning—indicating to her that the as-yet-unknown date of her marriage to Paul was indeed getting closer.

"We might as well forget about replacing your refrigerator with another small unit," Paul told her. "I have a small one, also. So what we'll do instead is buy an extra large model, and you'll keep it until we get married."

When the deliverymen were removing her old refrigerator, Mary Ann felt like a part of her past was going out the front door with it.

"Melissa and I found that refrigerator in an alleyway two blocks from here," Mary Ann recalled. "A neighbor helped us push it home on a small hand truck, and then the girls and I spent all weekend cleaning it up."

Paul did make one other offer to Mary Ann that she quickly turned down.

"An executive-director at my bank is looking for a cat," Paul mentioned. "If you want to give away one of your three, she would have a good home. In fact, it would be a very rich home, really. They have servants, and the cat could probably ring for her dinner every night."

"Absolutely not," Mary Ann countered. "They're all family, too. I couldn't part with any one of them. Four daughters, one husband, and three cats. That's all I want. And that's final."

However, a segment of Mary Ann's life that was definitely due to disappear concerned her unemployment status. A sudden but pleasant event took place just about the time the weather starts getting hot again in Pottstown—the middle of May.

First thing one sunny morning, Mary Ann received a phone call telling her that she had been hired.

"Good news," she phoned Paul. "Your fiancée is on the road to sanity again."

⬯

For the remainder of that balmy spring weekend, Melissa devoted a great deal of concentrated thought to Uncle Steve's "Go To Florida" suggestion. But at the end of much deliberation, she still wasn't sure if she had the nerve to do it. For her, such an action would constitute a definite change in character, sort of like assuming the male-dominant role in a courtship.

Just as a young man might fear that his request for a date with a woman would end in rejection, so did Melissa feel vulnerable at the prospect of asking Joe to pack up his Florida bags and move north with her.

In essence, whether or not she'd adhere to Uncle Steve's urgings would be a tough decision, and one she felt she would have to make soon. So, Melissa took a mental pledge that she would force herself to act on the prospect of a Florida trip—yes or no, one way or the other—before the end of March.

Meanwhile, the center of her attention for the next few days would be Atlantic City—site of a convention for members of the Pennsylvania State Librarians Association. Melissa was a member in good standing and a regular attendee of all association functions.

"It's ironically amusing," Melissa reflected, "that ever since casino gambling became legal in New Jersey, the Pennsylvania librarians, like groupies attracted to a rock band, have always trekked out-of-state, to Atlantic City, for their annual get-together. Such is the drawing power of a boardwalk full of wagering emporiums."

Melissa had to admit, though, that the casino city's electric atmosphere had never resulted in a dull convention.

The big town by the Jersey shore had changed quite a bit since she was a child. Melissa remembered fondly those occasions when her mom and stepfather would take her and her three sisters to Atlantic City or Ocean City—usually on weekends during the summer. It got so that Melissa knew the name, strength, and peculiarities of every diving horse at the famous Steel Pier. In this day and age, however, Atlantic City was less a family-type resort and more a conventioneer's city that also lured degenerate gamblers. Each group was attracted to night-long action at the green felt tables. The popularity of day trips in the family car for sunshine and ocean bathing had been replaced by day trips in a casino bus for blackjack and slot machine gambling.

When she checked in at her hotel, Melissa was glad to have a room on a lower floor. Sleeping on upper floors always disturbed her. She recalled when her stepfather had installed a metal, fire/security hook outside the window of her second floor room back when she was in junior high school. She had kept a connecting hook, attached to a long rope, under her bed. She never had to use it as a method of emergency escape, but it was still there when she'd left home for college.

On her first night in town for the convention, and in advance of three straight days of planned professional seminars, Melissa attended a retirement party for Olga Hines, one of the associate directors of the Philadelphia Free Library.

The meeting room for the librarians, in an anteroom right off the main lobby of the hotel, was decorated with photos of old Carnegie-façade libraries where Olga had worked, photos of a young Olga standing in front of old libraries, and photos of groups of librarians—some even older than Olga—with whom she had labored through the course of some forty-odd years.

Olga herself seemed overwhelmed by all the attention she was receiving from her co-workers. Petite, with short gray hair and eyeglasses that seemed too large for her face, Olga looked fit—and typecast—for the role of a cartoon-character librarian. The only missing prop would be a sign in her hand that said "Quiet Please."

One of the rumors circulating among the Philadelphia-area librarians was that Melissa might eventually be chosen to replace Olga. Melissa knew that she had a realistic chance for this step upward in the librarian hierarchy, but she wasn't campaigning actively for such a career promotion.

"If I get it, I get it," was her philosophy. "True, it might mean more money and more prestige for me, but it would also mean more administrative work. I'm kind of happy as a reference librarian. Finding answers to other people's questions is something that never gets boring."

Throughout the course of the evening's cocktail party and dinner, Melissa spent the better part of an hour or more talking with Jane Doherty, a long-time reference librarian who worked in a small South Philadelphia branch. And it was one of the stories Jane related that set the tone for the rest of Melissa's week in Atlantic City.

"I thought for awhile that I might have to retire prematurely from my library," Jane explained, "even though I really want to keep working for as long as I can. My husband, who was a Philadelphia city policeman, suffered a slight back injury and was forced into premature retirement a few years ago.

"After sitting around the house for only a month, though, the inactivity started to bother him, so we discussed the possibility that maybe I should retire, too, in order to keep him company. And I would have done it, just to make him happy, except that through a bit of luck, he stumbled into a full-time job that he just loves. He's a security consultant now for a casino that's just a few blocks away from here."

"Security? What does he do exactly?"

"He says it's just like the police work he did for most of his career. He supervises the guards on the casino floor, watches out for thieves and con men, and, occasionally, he arrests people."

"How dangerous is this job?" Melissa continued, her inquisitiveness genuine.

"From what he tells me, it's a lot easier than being a big-city cop. Basically, there are no street corner brawls or knife-wielding weirdos to worry about. And, so far, there have been no murders, no beatings, and no rapes on the casino floor.

"Most of the time he deals with purse snatchers, pickpockets, prostitutes, rich and poor types alike who deal in stolen goods, and counterfeiters.

"At least once a month someone tries to counterfeit those black chips that are used at the gambling tables. They're the ones worth a hundred dollars apiece."

"I don't mean to get too personal," Melissa again interjected, pursuing the matter further, "but tell me, Jane, since your husband is a retiree, wasn't there a problem with his age? The reason I'm asking is that a friend of mine has been looking for police work in the Philadelphia area, and he's gotten nowhere. He thinks it's because he's too old."

"Oh, no. They were happy to have him—considering all of his experience. In fact, he tells me that most of the casinos have hired ex-policemen for the security positions—or for the armed guard jobs. And as far as our personal relationship goes, his new work has just been great for us.

"Really, it's almost unbelievable, Melissa," Jane concluded, "but for the first time since we were married, over thirty years ago, my husband has a certain pride in his job title. He likes being referred to as a 'professional'—just like me. In the eyes of the world, he's no longer just a cop. He's been transformed—into a suit-and-tie-wearing consultant. For all those years when he was a cop, he probably felt inferior to me, but no more. I can't believe how this new job has changed him. He's lively, spirited, and seems to feel so good about himself."

For the remainder of the retirement party that evening, Melissa was present in body but not in mind. Outwardly, she may have appeared to be conversing normally with those around her, but inwardly her thoughts were dominated by visions of Joe obtaining a security consultant's position with the local casino industry, similar to the job that Jane's husband enjoys so much.

"If Joe got a job here, we could buy a house in southern New Jersey," she told herself, "halfway between Philly and Atlantic City. Getting a place in a location near where Uncle Steve lives would be perfect—about forty minutes drive time either way."

The following morning, Melissa opted to pass up attending two library seminars for which she had enrolled. Instead, she managed to visit every casino on the Atlantic City boardwalk, picking up employment applications for Joe at each stop along the way.

As she walked from one casino's personnel department to another, Melissa also found time to write a pocketful of notes that would be of value in Joe's job search—such as the names of key employees to whom he could address his resumes.

In what amounted to a full day's work, Melissa also spent several hours wandering through the gaming areas of each casino. Her purpose was to check out the doings of the security people on the floor and to try to get a feel for what it would be like for Joe to work in a gambling hall.

What startled her the most were the large numbers of women she saw.

"There seem to be just as many younger women sitting calmly at blackjack tables as there are older women frantically playing the slot machines," she wondered, almost aloud. "I never realized that this fascination for casino gambling included women to such a great extent. I'm not sure where I'd fit, though. Maybe I'm too old for the tables and too young for the machines!"

And even though Joe had never told her whether or not he liked to gamble in casinos as opposed to racetracks, Melissa felt confident that he would enjoy working in a gambling atmosphere—what with his affinity for wagering on horses and dogs.

During her travels around town, Melissa saw a bevy of armed guards that were a noticeable presence in just about every casino.

"These places are sort of like banks," she reasoned. "I imagine if there weren't so many guards standing around, looking tough, a lot more people would get tempted by all that money floating around in the open."

Before the one hundred dollar bills were exchanged for betting chips, these large denominations flashed briefly almost everywhere. Quickly, the dealers would stuff this cash downward through openings in the tables. And, occasionally, some of the bills would require extra shoves before they disappeared, as if they were objecting to the downward destination, like so many fish trying unsuccessfully to swim upstream.

The volume of dollars amazed Melissa at first. She realized, however, that in a casino, the money, after awhile, seems to lose its real meaning.

"That's why they use the chips," a bystander explained to her. "When people lose their chips, it doesn't seem as monumental or as traumatic as losing real money. Chips are like toys. The buying power in food, rent, or whatever just disappears when twenty-five American dollars become one tiny, green piece of plastic."

For her remaining days in Atlantic City, Melissa struggled mentally, alternating her brain power between snatches of professional duty and ideas for Joe. She did present herself at several seminars and at a workshop that analyzed "The Techniques and Record-Keeping Methods For Dealing With Reference Questions Received Via Telephone."

As soon as she returned to Philadelphia at the end of the week, Melissa wasted little time in getting straight back to her office in the library—for a bit of personal research.

During a three-hour, non-stop stretch, she dug into the guts of every casino management book and newspaper article she could find in order to ferret out kernels of information that would be helpful to Joe.

All told, she photocopied almost two dozen pages that Joe could use to brief himself on the ins-and-outs of how casinos are operated.

This, together with the piles of employment applications, the names of contacts in casino personnel departments, and the notes that she'd accumulated from her walking tour represented Melissa's total stack of readables.

She was confident that these materials could serve their purpose. Her beloved Joe would now have a head start on any job shopping he might get into while touring the East Coast's version of casino heaven.

"After all," she told herself, while admiring her casino information collection, "when I take Uncle Steve's advice and travel to Islamorada to claim my man, I might need more ammunition than my body and my smile."

Chapter 13

Although the pay wasn't outstanding, the job itself was one that Mary Ann had fantasized about for years.

"Finally, someone is willing to take a chance and train me," she voiced, excitedly, when describing her new position to Paul and the girls. "I'm going to be a Medical Assistant, a real Medical Assistant, working for three doctors. I'll learn to do blood pressure tests, take venipunctures, EKGs, medical records, the whole works. And I get to wear a white uniform, too. I've never, ever, worn a uniform before.

"Do you realize that this will be the first time I've had a job that's more than just a job? I might even be able to call myself a professional."

Without a doubt, Mary Ann felt that her long years of experience in administering to the girls' asthma problems had helped her to impress her employment interviewers.

"When we started talking about asthma drugs—the theophylline, the prednisone, the saline solutions—they could tell I was no dummy. I guess my interest in the medical field was what won them over."

Mary Ann had about an hour's drive to her new place of employment. The medical office, just south of Reading, was the farthest she'd ever had to travel to get to work.

"Since we've started seeing each other regularly," she told Paul, "I've gotten into the routine of shaving my legs every other night. That habit will save me time now, because I'll have to get up extra early every morning to get ready for my job."

Mary Ann was glad she had a new car.

"I can avoid the problems I used to have when I was poor," she reflected, thanking Paul once again for the Ford mini-wagon. "I'd often get car troubles and be late for work. Now, what with driving on the turnpike every day, the new car is really a blessing.

"I remember those long trips on the turnpike a few years ago, and how tough it was with my old car."

"Every two weeks, I'd drive the girls to a psychologist in Adamstown. He specialized in working with asthmatics, helping them adjust to their childhood years—you know, with the limited physical activity. I was lucky I didn't have any boys. I can't imagine telling a boy he can't play football or basketball.

"Really, I don't know if those sessions helped the girls or not, but I'd do the whole thing over again for them, even though it wasn't cheap. I guess I'm a mother first, with all else last."

Once Mary Ann started working steadily, she got to spend less time with the girls.

It was during one of those daily commutes in her car that she glanced to her right and saw four pennies sitting on the front passenger's seat.

"We put them there, Mommy," Melissa informed, "for good luck on your long drives. You can pretend that the pennies are the four of us, sitting next to you, helping you watch the road."

Paul, too, was concerned about the endless, tiring hours that Mary Ann spent commuting.

"I know you love your job," he told her. "But I don't like the fact that you're coming home exhausted every night. Let's do something daring, love, like moving out of Pottstown."

"But Paul, what about your job? You're not going to quit the bank, are you?"

"No. Not at all. And I'm not going to tell you to quit your job either. We'll compromise. Let's look for a house about halfway between where you work and where I work. Why should I be the one with just a five-minute commute every morning? I won't mind a bit of extra travel. If we move, it would be like I was sharing the driving with you.

"I can't think of a better way to start out a lifetime partnership."

∞

Melissa could never have done it without an overabundant store of confidence.

Deciding to surprise Joe by popping in unannounced in Islamorada appeared to be an unrealistic alternative when she first heard the suggestion from the lips of Uncle Steve.

But now that she possessed that heavy pile of job information on casino security positions, Melissa felt well fortified, and hence better able to embark on her journey for Joe's heart. Also, she reasoned, living with Joe Carlton for the rest of her life was a goal well worth chasing.

"And even if he turns me down," she reasoned, realistically, "it will be better for me to have found out right away. For the longer that a relationship goes on, the harder it is to forget."

Melissa's trip to Islamorada would be completely unexpected—as far as Joe was concerned. He would have no idea she was coming until she walked up to his trailer and knocked on the door. When she tried to picture that critical moment in her mind, Melissa's negative thoughts ranged from seeing Joe in bed with another woman to finding his trailer gone with only an empty lot at the site.

As were the arrangements with her most previous visit, Melissa took a plane directly to Miami. She chose a different airline this time and was disappointed when her on-board "snack" arrived—one lonely bag of peanuts.

"I guess," she snickered, "this outfit gives you macadamia nuts if you fly first class." Still, a more substantial meal would have given her a few minutes respite from her racing mind. Without it she just felt like a bundle of nerves.

At the airport in Miami, she rented a car and then began driving southwestward toward the Keys.

While enroute, she pulled into a rest area on the Florida Turnpike and recalled those occasions from her childhood when her stepfather would stop the family car at turnpike rest areas and buy lollipops for her and her sisters.

"Now, whenever I stop on the turnpike, I check out the condom machines in the lavatories. I wonder," she mused, "if I will soon be one of the women who needs to keep a condom handy. If this doesn't work out with Joe, I would be foolish not to. Sex these days is just too dangerous!"

Melissa thought ahead to the room she had booked at the Seascaper for three nights, hoping she would need much less time—a day at the most—to convince Joe that he should move north with her.

When she checked in at the Seascaper, Melissa was feeling somewhat like the typically honest citizen who was about to break the law for the very first time. It was an eerie feeling—a nervous sensation akin to being half inebriated and half worried that the world was about to laugh in her face. She fought back these mental uncertainties, however, and toted her bags into a beachfront room at about four o'clock in the afternoon. Somehow the soft yellows and blues of the drapes and the bedspread helped to have an immediate calming effect, as though she could feel the warmth of a bright sunny day right in her room.

Methodically, she refreshed herself with a shower and then shaved her slightly tanned legs until they were shiny and smooth.

"When a woman shaves her legs as often as I do," Melissa admitted, "it's a sure sign she's experiencing an ongoing relationship with a man. I hope, deep down, that this isn't the last time I shave them for awhile."

Melissa then stood erect in the center of the room to practice her sales pitch—just one more time prior to the real thing.

"I've got to be assertive," she acknowledged, while pointing to her own reflection in the oblong mirror that was hung above the dresser.

Melissa knew, from experience, that her blood would always pump faster if she could practice a speech while looking at herself in a mirror. The side-to-side movement of her head and body that she could follow with her eyes seemed to bring out the saleswoman in her—upbeat and forever on. It was a trait that would normally be locked deep within her psyche. Right now, she felt she needed it more than ever.

"We have to stop making excuses, Joe," she practiced, leaning on the word "we" and thus appearing to take part of the blame for the procras- tination that was Joe's alone.

"We're not the kind of people who should sit back and let events control us. We should be the ones who control the events.

"Both of us are mature adults who should know what's best for us. Let's do the right thing and make a commitment to spend the rest of our lives together."

So, with her speech preparations concluded, Melissa gave a quick sec- ond glance to her crisp white shirt and navy slacks, applied just a hint of lipstick, and marched off to find her man.

Walking through the early evening breezes toward her car, she seemed to exude the calm confidence of a tough but fair schoolteacher who was about to address a new class—or the steely reserve of a combat officer leading a squadron of soldiers into enemy territory.

Melissa, like either of the above, would be lying if she professed to have a stomach free of butterflies.

The narrow road toward Joe's trailer was bordered on both sides by dense tropical vegetation, making access seem even more restricted. As she approached, Melissa looked for lights inside the brown-façade structure, but she could quickly see that none were shining.

And after knocking on his door for about five minutes without getting a response, she concluded, obviously, that Joe wasn't home.

Inwardly, she cursed the fact that she wouldn't be able to talk to him at home. For at that very moment, she knew exactly what she wanted to say and was as high on confidence as she'd ever be. These were the reasons, she realized, that she must venture off immediately to the Islamorada police station. And no, she couldn't wait for Joe to come home after his work shift. She must seek him out—now.

Police headquarters in Islamorada consisted of a small, stucco building situated alongside the town hall. In fact, it looked like the town hall's garage. When she entered, she saw no other policemen except a solitary uniformed dispatcher on duty.

"Joe? Joe Carlton?" the man answered, in response to Melissa's query. "Joe took some vacation time just yesterday. I think he went to Key West for a few days."

Crushed was the only word to describe Melissa's feelings at that exact moment. Visions sped through her head of Joe escorting some wide-eyed female tourist through all of the Key West spots that they had visited so memorably just a short time ago.

Melissa strode outside and stood in the moonlight, perplexed and angry. She realized that Joe and his mystery woman might be holding hands somewhere nearby, perhaps on a beach or next to a pool. Or maybe they were gambling at the dog track—or were even in bed together, enjoying each other's laughter, each other's touch.

Deeply disappointed and in somewhat of a mental fog, Melissa still managed to drive back safely to her motel room.

Once inside, she sat down on the bed and tried hard to come up with a sensible decision. With her rental car, she could certainly drive to Key West and retrace the guided tour that Joe had given her. If he were, indeed, in the company of his "date," he would probably be taking her to most of those same romantic places in Key West, the places where Melissa and Joe experienced their first love—and their first true caring for each other.

The more she thought, though, the more she hated the prospect of going to Key West on her own. Such a choice appeared to have all the earmarks of a cut-and-dried, no-win situation.

For if she were to find Joe, escorting a woman, especially if it were a younger woman, her heart would certainly be broken. And, in the alternative, if she did not find him in Key West, her total time spent in that quaint, artsy city would be a complete downer, with nothing but unshared memories and countless visual reminders of happier times.

While she continued to sit on the edge of her bed, Melissa stared blankly at the wind-whipped, dancing palm fronds just outside her patio window.

For what seemed like the longest time, she tried to move but couldn't. As well, the act of thinking clearly seemed to be an even harder chore. Crying seemed her only alternative, and soon her chest and throat ached from the sobs that racked her small frame.

Eventually exhausted, Melissa reclined on the bed, her unseeing eyes now facing upward toward a dull, gray ceiling. After she had fallen asleep for perhaps half an hour, the ringing of the telephone awakened her. She was still groggy when she answered with a muffled, "Hello, who is it?"

"Melissa? You sound like you just woke up. This is Cammie, from the library," the voice reported. "Remember? You asked me to relay your messages. Well, you got a call here a little while ago. It sounded important. Are you awake enough to understand me?"

"Oh, I'm all right, Cammie," Melissa responded, slowly regaining her mental clarity, and reaching for the Kleenex to clear her stuffed up nose. "Who called?"

"Your friend, Joe Carlton. He didn't leave much of a message at all except the phone number where you can reach him. He did say he'd like to talk to you as soon as possible."

"Wait, let me get a pen . . . go ahead."

"It's a New Jersey number . . ."

After she scribbled down the digits, Melissa realized that the phone number in the message belonged to Joe's Uncle Steve.

"Could it be that Joe was actually staying at his uncle's place, only a few miles away from Philadelphia?" Melissa wondered. "It must be so. The phone number he left with Cammie confirms it."

"Did you tell him that I'm in Florida?" Melissa asked of Cammie.

"No," Cammie responded. "You told me not to tell anybody, remember?"

After thanking Cammie for the message and uttering a sincere good-bye, Melissa started, without warning, to laugh out loud—while still holding onto the phone.

"I don't believe it," she screamed, to no one in particular. "What could Joe possibly be doing at Uncle Steve's house?"

Dialing Uncle Steve's number proved a real joy. Melissa smiled and hunched over the phone like a little girl with bubble gum in her cheeks and a big secret ready to roll off her lips.

Not surprisingly, it was Joe who answered, and, almost immediately, the words started falling out of Melissa's mouth as quickly as dice leaving the hands of a craps shooter.

"Guess where I am, go ahead, guess. I dare you. Just take a wild guess."

"From the way you're laughing, Melissa, I'd have to say that you're calling from a singles bar after having had too many margaritas. Either that, or you just hit the millionaire lottery."

"No, silly. What if I told you that just a little while ago I talked, in person, to a gray-haired policeman, in a station house surrounded by palm trees? I was informed that a certain Officer Joe Carlton has probably gone off to Key West for a few days."

"What?"

"That's right, I'm in Islamorada—in a room at the Seascaper."

"That . . . that's amazing. And it was my idea to surprise you!" Joe revealed, his tone indicating obvious bewilderment. "What are you trying to do by coming down to see me? . . . No, don't answer that.

"Instead, listen for a second, Melissa," he stated, abruptly. "I'm sorry if what I'm about to say might seem to be out of place, but I'm afraid I can't just stop laughing about how you're in Florida, and I'm in Jersey. If I laugh, I might forget what I wanted to say.

"You see, the reason I called you at the library is that I've got to tell you something important right away, so don't you say anything until I'm finished, okay?"

"Uh, okay."

"I flew north for one reason—to see you in person, Melissa. I wanted to apologize for being such a fool and to ask you if we could set a definite date to get married.

"I really would like to move to Philly and to be with you permanently—as soon as possible—if you'll have me."

Hard pressed to hold back her unseen tears of happiness, Melissa answered in the affirmative.

"Of course I'll have you, you big, lovable thing, you.

"Now, Officer Carlton, don't you want to know what I'm doing in Islamorada?"

"Sure."

"I came down here to talk to you, Joe Carlton, because I missed you. I missed seeing your smile and having you hold me."

"Melissa, I realize now that you're the best thing that has ever happened to me. Your past, my past, they're immaterial. And I hope you'll forgive me for being so casual with your emotions. Ever since I've met you, Melissa, it's been like a new life for me. You've been responsible for how confident and well adjusted I've felt in the past few months. I'm sure of that now."

"And as for my feelings," Melissa told him, "I don't give two hoots about your not having a college degree. Even if you were a third-grade dropout, I'd love you just because you're you."

"Let's stop talking, Melissa," Joe concluded, "so that I can get on the first plane back to Florida.

"As soon as I say good-bye to Uncle Steve, I'll quit this cold weather. Just tell me your room number at the Seascaper. And I don't care what the Islamorada gossips might say. The way I'm feeling now, I'll park a submarine in front of your door."

⚬

The following afternoon, as soon as Joe arrived in Florida, he and Melissa made furious, passionate love to one another.

Their coupling was accented by stronger than usual embraces, as if the power of their feelings was being expressed by heavy arms clutching warm bodies—bodies that now held carefree, unburdened hearts.

"Making love to someone who cares for me as much as I care for him is the greatest feeling in the world," Melissa realized. "In some ways, Joe is like the guardian angel who has been sitting next to me for all of my life. Suddenly, I'm able to reach out and communicate, physically, with that angel."

Afterwards, they headed for the sunny outdoors to catch the rays alongside the reflected warmth of the Seascaper pool.

As sunset neared, and they saw that the last of the other guests had gone, they entered the glistening waters. And while submerged neck-high in the blue-clear water, they slipped out of their swimsuits to continue their frolic in ultra-cool surroundings.

Feeling Joe's strength as she watched those sun-colored waters rippling in concert with the motion of their bodies succeeded in lifting Melissa to a new plane of physical and mental satisfaction.

By the end of their mini-vacation, she and Joe had completed three full days in Islamorada, days when they did nothing except soak up the sun—and each other.

Their one excursion out of town during this period provided a strange interlude. They were boat passengers on a brief nighttime frogging expedition among a group of mangrove islands and swamps that border the northern edge of Key Largo.

The trip was taken on the insistence of Moira O'Grady, the friendly, ebullient woman who ran the Islamorada Chamber of Commerce office.

"Mrs. O'Grady's husband has been giving these frogging tours for almost twenty years now," Joe told Melissa. "Both of them have been egging me on to take one for a long time now."

And, overall, Melissa wasn't disappointed, calling her escorted search for frogs the "spookiest and most insane evening" she'd ever spent outdoors.

"The frogs make such a deep, foreboding sound, amplified by the water's surface," she noted. "In the complete darkness, they can easily be mistaken for unseen monsters hundreds of times their size."

Melissa was relieved, also, to find that the frogs weren't captured with the intent that their legs become entrées in local restaurants. All of them, even the biggest—at a length of about a foot—were released after spending scant seconds aboard the boat.

On their final night in Islamorada, Melissa and Joe decided to dine at the Whale House Restaurant, which featured a décor of hanging wooden plaques that bore memorable mottoes and recognizable literary quotes.

Appropriately, on the island full of whistling palm fronds, their table was situated just to the left of John Masefield's line, "where the wind's like a whetted knife" and directly below Longfellow's famous description of "ships that pass in the night."

"We passed each other in the air, didn't we?" Melissa offered.

"Never again," Joe toasted, hoisting a glass of Chablis. "As of this day, our independence is equal, but our hearts, and our souls, will always fly together."

Chapter 14

"I'm going to miss being a part of this town," Mary Ann commented, as she and Paul watched the movers hustling in and out of her apartment. "Pottstown will always seem like home to me, especially at this time of year. I love the summer smell of barbecues, the walks along the creek, and watching the kids still playing on the sunlit streets long after suppertime."

"Do you remember much of anything," Paul offered, "about when you moved into this place?"

"Oh, we rented a truck and did it ourselves," Mary Ann noted, "like most people do, I guess, when they have to watch their money. After we got all of the big furniture in the truck, we piled our clothes on top of everything. Then we hoped the truck would start. It really wasn't so bad, but I'm not sure I have the energy to undertake a move like that again."

"Well, as long as I have something to say about it, you won't have to ever move like that again," Paul commented while squeezing Mary Ann around the shoulders.

The new house that Mary Ann and Paul had selected was a spacious colonial that contained four bedrooms and a recreation area—extra living space that would require more furniture. It also had a two-car garage.

"I know how you love to shop," Paul laughed. "So it shouldn't take us too long to fill up all the rooms."

Paul noticed that Mary Ann was carrying her small, fish-shaped pillow with her during the move.

"Some things you just don't trust to the movers," she explained. "I go to sleep hugging this pillow every night. 'Rainbow' is almost as dear to me as the cats.

"I am worried about one other thing, though. With all the traveling I've been doing back and forth to work, I've been lucky to lose a few pounds. I hope I don't put the weight back on now since I have only a twenty-minute drive. If I edge up over 140 again, it'll be up to you, Paul, to cut off my ice cream supply.

"And I suppose I am relieved that this isn't a big, cross-country move. I'll still be close enough if I want to visit my old friends.

"Anyhow, when you still have stuff on layaway at three different department stores, you just can't move too far, can you?"

When Paul was taking out a handful of $100 bills to pay the moving men, Mary Ann uttered what had become one of her standard, joking comments.

"Whenever I see a roll of money like that, I get more and more convinced that you and those cats have a secret printing press in a basement somewhere."

One of the features of the new house that caught Paul's eye was the fact that it was situated less than two miles from an amusement park.

"You like roller coasters and carousels almost as much as the girls do," Paul commented. And Mary Ann's quick smile told him he was right.

Soon after they'd arrived at their new house—before they'd even started to unpack—Mary Ann, Paul, and the girls drove over to the amusement park to check out the rides.

However, when they pulled into the lot near the front gate, a sudden thunderstorm prevented them from leaving the car.

"Look, Paul," Mary Ann pointed, as they stared through the windshield into dark clouds and a horizon splattered with lightning. "It's starting to hail. The hail is bouncing off the kids' water slides, making a pinging sound. It looks like God is cooking popcorn. It even sounds like it."

"I hope this rain on our first day at the new house isn't a bad sign," Paul offered, forlornly.

"Nope, this place is perfect," Mary Ann countered. "When I was walking in the backyard a few minutes ago, I found this . . ."

Reaching into her purse, she pulled out what looked to Paul like a small, green weed.

"It is," Mary Ann smiled, confidently, "a four-leaf clover."

For Joe Carlton, it wasn't one of the easiest chores in the world to say good-bye to Islamorada.

True, for the rest of his life he wouldn't have to contend with southern Florida's innumerable hurricane threats—and the fears of being swallowed by tidal waves or hoisted into the air by one-hundred-mile-per-hour winds.

But he had made a host of friends and acquaintances on this small tropical island, and for Joe, the loss of sympathetic companionship would always be painful.

His co-workers in the police department with whom he had served, side-by-side, and the cheerful island residents whom he had grown to know on a first-name basis were all saddened by the news of his impending relocation to Philadelphia.

Most typical of the feelings expressed locally were the words of Jack Fidati, the service station operator in town who was always ready with a kind word and a cup of hot coffee when Joe would drive in to say hello during his rounds.

"Islamorada will be losing a good person and a good cop," Fidati told Joe, shaking his hand warmly "But since this little town is such a fantastic place to visit, we know you'll be back for the spectacular sunshine and the friends you've made here."

Joe's buddies on the police force all wished him the best of luck and offered to provide whatever job references and letters of recommendation he might need in order to find new work.

"I guess the one thing I'll miss the most about Islamorada," Joe reflected, "is waking up with my bedroom window open and experiencing a warm and cozy feeling. The blessings of the weather made going to work every day so much easier.

"It was nice—it was very nice here. But now, like the tides that have come and gone at my doorstep, it is time I moved on.

"Melissa and I are definitely coming back, perhaps on a regular basis, chasing our sacrament of sea and sun," he announced—to just about everyone. "For we realize that this island will always be an important part of us."

Melissa enjoyed having Joe as a permanent house guest in Philadelphia.

Aside from the love that they shared every day and the contentment that Melissa always experienced while in his company, their living arrangement also had its practical benefits.

No longer did Melissa have to throw together those hastily designed, freezer-fresh dinners—for herself and her most finicky critic, Coke.

Since Joe genuinely enjoyed preparing food, he spent every weekday afternoon as the cook-in-residence in Melissa's ample kitchen.

And on those mornings when he had no scheduled job interviews, he would tackle the various housecleaning chores and the shopping.

In essence, and to Melissa's delight, he was the consummate "house husband."

Meanwhile, on that heretofore frustrating employment front, Joe was starting to receive a great amount of positive feedback—especially from his job hunting in Atlantic City.

"All told now, four casinos have interviewed me," Joe told Melissa, some two weeks after they had started living together.

"In every case I felt well-accepted, as if they appreciated the time I took to apply. I've talked with personnel administrators as well as with heads of security departments. And I don't think I'm boasting when I say that everyone seemed impressed with my background and abilities.

"Of course, it could be that some of those people were just fooling me with plastic kindness, but I don't think so. I believe I really came across effectively.

"And you know, it feels good to be respected for what I've accomplished so far in my life. My self-esteem is higher now than ever before."

Regarding her wedding preparations, everything that Melissa did—from phone calls, to shopping, to the writing of the invitations—seemed to maintain her bubbly feeling of constant joy.

Despite the fact that Joe, as of yet, had no firm employment commitment, the two of them were proceeding steadily with their nuptial plans, oblivious to any possible monetary problems that might materialize in the future.

"I feel like I'm living my youth all over again," Melissa beamed, while relaxing at home on the sofa one evening, talking to an audience composed of Joe, who had fallen asleep during a television game show, and Coke, who was sitting on top of the stereo, saying nothing.

"The excitement of contracting for the photographer, figuring out the seating chart, and talking with the minister—the whole thing is like an infusion of caffeine. It's all quite time-consuming, but I'm loving every minute.

"Now I know," she smirked, "why some women enjoy getting married over and over again. The anticipation is truly exhilarating. It's the same way I felt back in high school when I was getting ready for my first prom—daydreaming and getting high on music with every twirl of my hairbrush.

"I'm in such a positive frame of mind now that I wouldn't be surprised at all if the gray follicles on my head started going in reverse, turning me absolutely brown again."

As to future living arrangements, Melissa and Joe were sticking to their original plan, which consisted of finding a place that was equidistant between their job locations.

Of course, with Atlantic City now the likely area of Joe's employment, they were targeting a move to one of the towns in southern New Jersey—about halfway between Melissa's library and Joe's casino.

Just as Melissa had speculated long ago in their relationship, a locale somewhere near Uncle Steve's house would be ideal.

And while Joe himself was feeling nothing but positive vibes as to his promising employment leads, Melissa's own job picture was also brightening. Twice in the past month she had been questioned by her superiors, informally, as to whether she had any interest in assuming the duties of associate library director, the position that recent retiree Olga Hines had held for so many years.

Overall, the atmosphere surrounding Joe during this busy period was likewise upbeat. Being a house husband provided him with a refreshing break from his years of police work. As well, the prospect of landing a casino security job added immeasurably to his mental well-being.

And even though he didn't reap the same conscious thrill that Melissa seemed to experience from the seemingly hundreds of pre-nuptial preparations, there was one aspect of his pending marriage that brought a smile to his face whenever his thoughts centered on the subject—his wedding gift to Melissa.

Joe's choice consisted of a pair of white porcelain coffee mugs molded into the shape of swans, with their curved necks servings as cup handles. He had read that in nineteenth century Europe, swans were the preferred gift for newlyweds. The elegance of swans—especially in tandem—was seen as symbolic of marital bliss, since they are faithful, monogamous birds that will always suffer tremendous grief at the loss of a partner.

When Joe told Uncle Steve the history behind the gift of swans, Steve pointed out that a better-than-average intelligence level was necessary to key such a selection.

"The gift you chose for Melissa," Uncle Steve told him, "is one more bit of proof that you're not as dumb as your bulging muscles may make you look. College degree or not, you've showed your class. I would say that not too many of those friends of Melissa's you've told me about could put as much thought or knowledge into a gift as you have."

Uncle Steve, in fact, was also in the unique position of knowing exactly what Melissa had selected as her wedding gift to Joe.

"I took your advice," Melissa told Uncle Steve. "Binoculars and a calculator. He'll be the best equipped horse player ever to set foot on a racetrack."

To his credit, Uncle Steve made other notable contributions to the upcoming wedding. It was he who contracted for the reception hall.

"My long-time friend, Len Rossen, has one of the neatest and best-looking places in all of Camden County," Uncle Steve told his favorite couple. "You can leave it to Len to make sure that every detail is taken care of."

Uncle Steve also arranged for the wedding day entertainment. Several members of his senior citizen club had formed a utensil band. Using only forks, knives, spoons, and glasses filled with water, they consistently struck up a delightful brand of music that was equal to or better than the much spiffier instrument bands—the kind that would have booked for five times as much money.

During the countdown to their wedding date, Melissa and Joe made a loyal practice of visiting Uncle Steve regularly every Sunday afternoon.

They would either bring along a high-caloric dessert to complement the dish that Uncle Steve was cooking or would visit a local restaurant with Uncle Steve as their guest.

On June 8th, only forty-one days before their wedding, Melissa and Joe were basking in their usual good spirits while driving into New Jersey for another Sunday with Uncle Steve.

Soon after they opened the door to his house, however, they realized that they would never be able to share the happiest day in their lives with the one person whom they both loved so dearly.

Sprawled on his living room floor, Uncle Steve lay dead—from a sudden heart attack.

In the kitchen at the same time, the dinner he had cooked was still bubbling in its containers.

Gone forever would be Sundays with Uncle Steve.

And although Melissa and Joe were equally distraught, it was Melissa who, in so short a time, had unexpectedly grown to love this kindly old man—much more than she could have imagined.

"No more sparkle in those clear, blue eyes. No more life in that wrinkled, infectious smile," she realized. "No more light-hearted Sundays, and no more luncheon visits alone when I could pour out my feelings to a man who seemed to understand so well."

Together in tears of sorrow for the first time, Melissa and Joe held onto each other tightly, continuing to weep for the longest period. They prayed for the soul of a man who had truly signified the word "family" for each of them—a man who had exemplified the meanings of care, compassion, and above all, joy.

Chapter 15

When Paul took off his sneakers, the unmistakable sound of Velcro fasteners punched the bedroom air. That 6 a.m. "swip, swip" sound had the same effect as an alarm clock—waking Mary Ann every morning that Paul returned from his sunrise jog.

After she awoke, Mary Ann would always spend another fifteen minutes or so lying in bed—staring at the ceiling and thinking. As her wedding date drew closer, she seemed to focus more and more on realizing that she was, indeed, a lucky woman.

A little over two years ago, she had her suicide note written, and she was ready to end it all. The bills she couldn't pay, her desire for the kids to have a better life than she could give them, the long hours at work, the loneliness at night after she put the girls to bed—all of those things played a part in how miserable she felt back then.

She burned that suicide note after she fell in love with Paul, but she could still see the letters and words of the last line she wrote, right above where she signed her name: "—I hope my kids will remember their Mom, wherever their dreams take them—"

She found it hard to believe that right now she was about to become a happily married lady.

"Those baby suits are a great idea," Paul interrupted, as he readied himself for work. "You're absolutely right. The girls mustn't feel left out. They should also get gifts on our wedding day."

Paul was referring to the infant-sized clothing that Mary Ann's daughters were wearing right after they were born—when they came home from the hospital. Mary Ann had saved these one-piece jumpsuits as well as all of the girls' nametag bracelets.

"It's time I gave them their baby clothes," Mary Ann told Paul. "They're old enough now to care about history, keepsakes, and mortality."

"Years from now," Paul noted, "when the girls look down at these tiny suits, they'll feel a wee bit humble. And when we're not around any more, the baby suits will help them remember us."

"Forget about us," Mary Ann added. "What's better for them is that they'll have a sense of where they came from. They'll need just one glance, and a few seconds of thought. That's all it will take."

❦

The sign read Golgotha Street, but there were no brownstones looming over early morning visitors, no children playing games, no adults scurrying past purposefully, with their minds attached to a daily agenda.

It was shortly after daybreak when Melissa and Joe visited the cemetery. Breathing the crisp morning air, they seemed to know in advance that their memories of this journey would, no doubt, stay vivid, long past the heat of summer.

The austere faces of headstones were standing in fast formation as they drove slowly past. They strained to read path signs such as Reunion Lane and Heavenly Highway.

Melissa was fighting the irresistible urge to scan as many surnames as possible—all screaming for attention in capital letters. She was so engrossed in this activity that she was unaware of a maintenance truck that crawled by in the opposite direction, billowing smoke.

Her feelings were lifted ever so slightly as she read those names—for they were other people's and definitely not hers. She was comfortable knowing she would never read the words "Melissa Carlton" carved forever in the indestructible stone. She wanted to touch those names, to run her fingers through the middle initials, much as she had done with the engravings on Islamorada's hurricane monument.

Continuing, Melissa then consumed each birth date she saw, comparing it with her own.

Joe stopped the car and turned off the ignition as they neared Lot 70, Row 7, Plot 52. Melissa thought that even in death, human beings are given a number. Perhaps this is the last one.

After hesitating for seconds that seemed like minutes, Melissa and Joe exited their car. Taking two wreaths of flowers, they walked up a slight, sod-covered incline. Melissa noticed how the dew-topped grass gave in readily beneath her shoes—just as the people below her had given in. The damp, pliant soil also echoed a death of all resistance.

Surrounding them were puddles from a recent rainfall. These tiny circles of water bounced rays of a resurging sun into her sleep-worn eyes before evaporating imperceptibly.

Then, suddenly, she saw it.

Uncle Steve's marker was small, imbedded at ground level. An adjacent grave, meanwhile, contrasted measurably—flaunting a huge, free-standing tablet.

Somehow, though, Melissa told herself, even the most impressive mausoleum can't disguise the reality of death. Death is a category the Taj Mahal would fail to elevate.

After sliding the spokes of their wreaths into the ground, Melissa and Joe bowed their heads for a few brief prayers, focusing their eyes on the marker. The year of Uncle Steve's death was starkly visible. It would never change.

"Instead of carvings that show us just the dates of someone's birth and death," Joe noted, "gravestones should indicate the periods of great personal accomplishment, like when battles were won or when children were born."

As she turned to leave, with her foot pushing ever so slightly into the turf, Melissa wondered if the weight of the earth had yet begun its task of crushing the casket below.

While walking away, Melissa carefully noticed the names of the people who were buried near Uncle Steve, just as a mother would warily screen the playmates of her children.

Almost every one of them, she reasoned, once flew about happily in life's formation, like sun-seeking, southbound swallows, before faltering, unexpectedly, alone.

Fortunately for Uncle Steve, the framed, smiling face on the mantelpiece in Melissa's home will never be able to watch his body turn to dust.

At that moment, Melissa remembered Uncle Steve telling her how he always loved to talk on the telephone, anytime, day or night.

"In some ways, being dead is like being poor," she told Joe. "It's as if Uncle Steve can't afford a phone now. But if he thinks he has to get in touch with us, he'll find a way—by pigeon, maybe."

On the stroll back to the car, Melissa noticed that two wooden staffs holding tiny American flags were implanted at an angle in a nearby grave, like banderillas that had been thrust poetically into the shoulders of a charging bull. The staffs sat curved and worn from the weather, Melissa surmised, remnants of a Memorial Day visit.

An image-laden Della Robbia wreath, holding its colorful fruit, graced one freshly turned gravesite, while a blanket of flowers lay on another. Soon, a rampaging summer greensward would cover both, spiced with weeds and growing long, spreading its quilt of oblivion.

Out of the corner of her eye, Melissa saw a bent, elderly woman, kneeling. The woman's face, and perhaps her thoughts, were hidden by a babushka. She crouched, like a broken-willed slave, having suffered from years, no doubt, of carrying widowhood's cross.

Almost immediately, Melissa knew the old woman's name, for it was lettered on her dead husband's stone. Her year of birth, a dash, and a blank. Melissa wondered, aloud, what the woman was praying for.

In their car now, Melissa and Joe motored toward the cemetery exit, where they waited for traffic to clear. They sat, idling under an ornate arch, beneath gates that are open to all.

"It would be nice," Melissa spoke, "if Uncle Steve could see them as heaven's gates."

From the time she arrived home later that morning, straight through until nightfall, Melissa thought of nothing else except her visit to the cemetery. Then, while lying in a darkened bed and once again wrapped in Joe's arms, she realized that she was not alone.

Chapter 16

The first Saturday in October brought sunny skies and Indian-summer warmth—as gorgeous a wedding day as Mary Ann or Paul could ever want. For this long-anticipated occasion, Mary Ann's "serious" gift to Paul consisted of a solid gold tie clasp in the shape of a horse's head.

On the lighter side, she also gave him a tape recording of snoring sounds—Paul's own.

"He has always denied that he snores when he's sleeping," she laughed. "Now he'll have the proof."

Mary Ann had already received her gift from Paul—several weeks in advance of the wedding.

"Maybe I shouldn't have given you those contact lenses," Paul told her, jokingly. "They make you look young enough to be my daughter."

The inspiration for the contact lenses originated shortly after they'd met. Mary Ann had accidentally broken her only pair of glasses, and Paul had quickly taken her to an optician who specialized in one-hour repair.

"Afterwards," Paul had revealed, "when you said, 'thanks, hon, I don't know how I'd be able to work without them,' it was the first time I'd ever felt like a true Good Samaritan. On that day, you needed help, and I was there to give it to you."

The job of decorating the reception hall on the night before the wedding had been accepted eagerly by Mary Ann and the girls.

"You know how I love to decorate," Mary Ann had revealed. "In just a few years, you'll be comfortable seeing witches and bats every Halloween, turkeys and pilgrims for Thanksgiving, snow stencils for Christmas, and party streamers for the girls' birthdays."

"This hall is really a nice place, except for the bathroom," Melissa had told her mom. "There's a nasty sign on top of the sink that says, 'Don't Put Paper Towels In The Toilet.' So, I took a crayon and wrote, 'Don't Put Any Blow Dryers In There Either.'"

Mary Ann couldn't help but think about community property again. Once married, she would legally be entitled to half of Paul's wealth. This contrasted starkly to the waning days of her previous marriage. Her former husband, Donald, had tricked her into signing bankruptcy papers shortly before he disappeared.

Mary Ann and Paul had finally decided on Hawaii for their honeymoon. Paul had helped her pick out the blue, pinstriped business suit that she would wear on the plane.

"It'll look great," he added, "especially when we land, and one of those beach boys puts multicolored leis around your neck."

In a break from tradition, Paul and Mary Ann walked down the aisle together, hand-in-hand, both wearing white.

"I don't have anything on that's old or blue," Mary Ann whispered, as they sat in the limousine, waiting to leave the churchyard.

"For tonight," she told her new husband, "I do have my Mom's sexy blue nightgown. It's even sexier now with all the big holes in it.

"And when we get to Hawaii, I'm going to decorate myself like a wedding gift. I'll wear nothing but balloons—and you can break them, one-by-one.

"When they explode, it'll get me in the mood—for some screaming."

∽

The wedding of Melissa and Joe succeeded in becoming a truly remarkable occasion. The fact that Uncle Steve wasn't in attendance, however, left a void that could never be filled.

Uncle Steve would have enjoyed the reception. It was his kind of party. During the cocktail hour, a piano player was able to handle all requests for oldies and even super oldies. He plunked the keyboard in a range of songs from 1940s show music to early rock, mixing in a little bit of country along the way.

And Uncle Steve would have loved the gourmet appetizers. Fresh figs, sliced kiwi fruit, and Armenian string cheese were all spread bountifully throughout the open-bar area. The main dish, too, would have put one more grin of enjoyment on that ever-friendly face of his.

This impressive entrée consisted of a scrumptious sampling of traditional Polish dishes, including kielbasa and cheese pierogis.

Also offered were hard-boiled eggs colored deep blue, with Easter-like designs on the shells.

"The eggs were my idea," Joe told Melissa. "Since I couldn't find any other blue food, I had to create some."

Earlier that morning, almost a hundred people had gathered to see Melissa and Joe exchange their vows at a small church just outside the Philadelphia city limits.

Melissa wore a long, mauve-shaded gown with white lace cuffs, a wide-brimmed, mauve-and-white veiled hat, and a loosely tied cincture that accentuated her taut waist.

Joe's tuxedo was a light, shiny gray, complete with high-backed tails, bow tie, and matching shoes. Melissa particularly admired the tight fit of his clothing. The suit, she thought, made Joe's body look slim, strong, and, above all, sexy.

At the conclusion of the brief religious ceremony, just about all of the churchgoing guests traveled a short distance across town to attend the reception.

Representing Melissa's family were her mother and stepfather, her three sisters, and a smattering of aunts, uncles, cousins, nieces, and nephews. Melissa's oldest sister served as matron of honor.

Since Joe's parents were both deceased, and with him an only child, his lone family tie was a cousin, Katy Kale, whom he hadn't seen in twelve years. Three of his Islamorada co-workers did make it, though, as did his closest buddy from the Marines—and best man—John Olivera, who was now a practicing dentist in Miami.

By far the biggest contingent was from several Philadelphia libraries. This group included Sylvia Smith, the mentor who had first hired Melissa.

The most unusual guests were the men who accompanied Melissa's former college roommates, Chris and Karen. These two blonde, well-dressed women, as similar as sisters, brought along their doting husbands, who were identical twins.

Several of the partygoers asked Melissa and Joe an expected question:

"How did you two meet?" And, in all, Melissa gave the "he saved me from a burning pier" speech exactly six times.

Melissa and Joe seemed to be smiling or joking throughout the entire evening. Long into the festivities, Joe still looked dashing in his gray tailored tuxedo, while Melissa's distinctive gown made her easily recognizable as the lady of the moment.

The utensil band proved extremely popular. Before the group started playing, however, they must have sensed an undercurrent of derogatory smirks and low-key laughter emanating from the crowd.

Carrying their kitchen tools—which served as unlikely looking musical instruments—this aging but proud assemblage of artists tottered onto the stage in a deliberate, almost mechanical fashion, seeming to smile and bow in unison as they faced their audience.

Although their instruments were of the same type, no two were exactly the same. This lack of uniformity gave the group an appearance akin to George Washington's fabled Continental Army—uneven and less than strong but motivated to succeed.

Not surprisingly, after they performed a remarkably well-tuned rendition of "Here Comes the Bride," those in attendance gave them an enthusiastic and truly sincere round of applause.

Soon, the tingling sound of metal-on-metal and the bell-like ringing of the water glasses gradually started to captivate almost all of the wedding guests. The listeners danced to old standbys such as "Daddy's Little Girl," "When Irish Eyes Are Smiling," and that all-time Philly favorite, "The Mummers Strut."

Later into the evening, Melissa and Joe were still at the reception hall, waiting for the last of the revelers to leave.

They themselves were in no real hurry to depart, since they'd decided, some time ago, to do without an immediate honeymoon. Joe's recent acceptance of a security consultant's position with a boardwalk casino necessitated that he begin work two days hence, on the Monday following their wedding.

As well, Melissa was only a week away from starting her expanded new duties as one of the Philadelphia Free Library's associate directors.

Their delayed honeymoon, which they were tentatively scheduling for the following winter, would consist of a week in Islamorada—supplemented by a one-night side trip to a new underwater motel in nearby Key Largo.

"I understand that you need scuba gear to get from this motel's parking lot to your room," Joe told Melissa.

"It's gong to feel weird in that underwater motel, looking out the window and seeing fish swim by," Melissa chuckled. "And taking a shower would seem a bit superfluous.

"But since we'll be spending most of our time in good old Islamorada, it sounds like a honeymoon that'll be well worth waiting for."

Melissa and Joe had both agreed to spend their actual wedding night at home in Philadelphia. And, when they finally got there, in concert with tradition, Melissa and Joe walked up to the front door and then stopped—so that Joe could carry her over the threshold and into the living room.

Placing Melissa on the sofa, he instructed her not to move while he quickly doubled back to lock the front door.

"Don't take too long," Melissa giggled, feeling the effects of a day dominated by champagne, white wine, and wedding cake.

"I'm starting to laugh from all of the drinks I've had," she continued, almost shouting now. "And when I laugh, I do crazy things."

Within seconds, Joe had jumped onto the couch next to Melissa. With hands that moved quicker than those of a professional prizefighter, he proceeded, deftly, to take off Melissa's clothes as well as his own.

Soon they were wrapped together in their nakedness, clutching each other feverishly—kissing, holding, and, before long, locking together passionately in their first lovemaking as man and wife.

"Did it feel any different, now that we're married?" Melissa asked Joe, afterward.

"Better," he answered, "much, much better. Maybe it's because there's a permanence to us now, don't you think?"

"I'm sure of only one thing," Melissa responded, right before she turned off the light and pulled an afghan over their exhausted bodies.

"We haven't been married for a full day yet—and I like it already."

"On Sunday, we go nowhere," Melissa had told Joe. "We stay at home and enjoy each other's company."

And so, they rose late the day after their wedding. From just past noon, they continued with their lovemaking straight through until almost dinnertime.

When they were finally ready for food, Joe remembered that Melissa had insisted on preparing a gourmet feast for that evening.

The dinner proved to be one of Melissa's best. She used a large skillet to fry a combination of fresh crabmeat and two different cheeses—Swiss and provolone. Vegetables consisting of asparagus spears and baked potatoes proved to be the perfect complement.

The dessert that followed was a true reminder of southern Florida—key lime pie. Melissa made it from scratch, using a bottle of fresh squeezed lime juice brought in directly from Islamorada by a wedding guest—one of Joe's fellow policemen who was more than happy to do the favor.

That Sunday alone in each other's company—which comprised their abbreviated honeymoon—ended all too quickly for Melissa and Joe. They could look forward, however, to their upcoming winter vacation, when they planned to do some extended celebrating in what they now considered their home away from home—Islamorada.

☙

In the weeks following their wedding, Melissa and Joe settled comfortably into a satisfying domestic routine.

For most of each week, both of them were working—but during daytime hours only. Their ample evenings left more than enough time for quiet dinners, walks through the neighborhood, and an occasional movie or play.

Melissa's new associate director's position proved to be an easy professional adjustment for her.

Joe's job may have required an hour of commuting each way, but the work itself seemed to fit him like the proverbial duck on a freshwater lake.

His experience with police work, coupled with his thorough knowledge of the world of gambling, resulted in an unbeatable combination—good for him, and better yet for his employer.

"We're concentrating now on thwarting the con men among us," he explained to Melissa one evening, while laughing heartily. "Some of the scams they're trying now were hustler angles that Uncle Steve showed me when I was still in high school. Your basic premise is that you've got to expect all of these characters to lie. A con man who tells the truth is a con man with no imagination. Those who show the greatest amount of ingenuity are the ones who work in groups. And they do manage to fool a few of our casino dealers. But our organization has also been blessed with a top-notch team of security people, one that does a good job of keeping two steps ahead of the cheaters."

About three months after they were married, Melissa and Joe scheduled an appointment with Wilton Butler, the lawyer who was handling Uncle Steve's estate. They had been told earlier by attorney Butler that Uncle Steve had willed his house to them. And after only a brief discussion between themselves, Melissa and Joe decided that Uncle Steve's old house would be a perfect spot to live.

On its own merits, the place appealed to them. Also, they realized that living in southern New Jersey, a bit closer to Atlantic City, would facilitate Joe's daily commute.

"This lawyer, Butler, was a friend of Uncle Steve's for over sixty years," Joe told Melissa. "Steve spoke to me more than once about the times he and Wilt Butler used to swim together in the Delaware River when they were kids, jumping off the tall cargo ships that had berthed at the old sugar factory in South Philly. Butler's a good guy. He'll make sure everything goes smoothly."

∽

Wilton Butler, although born in the same year as Uncle Steve, Joe had recalled, always looked to be considerably older. This wizened, almost bald barrister sported an oblong, clean-shaven head, save only for a few remaining clumps of white, bushy hair—all centered in front of his ears.

"Truncated sideburns," Butler called them.

He was a smallish man, still thin, and had a calculating appearance that belied the friendliness of the greeting.

"Welcome, newlyweds," he bellowed, in a voice that was a reminder, decibel-wise, of Uncle Steve's. "And pardon me if I ask you to repeat yourselves now and then. My hearing isn't what it used to be."

After Butler handed over the pile of documents, Joe noticed that they appeared to be in order—and surprisingly free of legalese.

And while her husband flipped through the pages, scanning paragraph after paragraph, Melissa could concentrate only on the little house in New Jersey that she would soon call home.

Melissa had liked Uncle Steve's rancher from the first time she saw it. In a pleasant, older neighborhood, it was fronted by large sycamores at curbside and was only a five-minute walk from a nearby shopping center.

"The backyard is beautiful," she remembered. "Joe told me that the giant oak tree in the middle of the lawn is almost forty years old. Uncle Steve transplanted it himself from the adjacent woods right after he first moved in. He was careful to remember which branches faced the sun in the tree's previous location, and he even used a compass to ensure that the replanting was exactly right. He was determined that the north side of that tree would still be facing north in its new home."

Another attraction at Uncle Steve's house was the large cultivated area where he had planted summer crops of tomatoes, peppers, cucumbers, and Brussels sprouts. There was even a small group of blueberry bushes that bore fruit every June.

"I think I signed my name everywhere that I was supposed to—on the correct dotted lines," Joe told the lawyer. "But don't ask me if I understood anything."

Butler flipped through the papers quickly, then he peered directly at Joe—from over the top of his half-circle reading glasses.

"I'll need Melissa's signature, too," he explained, mysteriously. And when he had finished speaking these words, Butler couldn't help but notice the surprised look on the faces of his visitors.

"While the remainder of Steve's estate was willed just to you, Joe," Butler continued, "he left the house to both you and Melissa, jointly.

"Even though, as we are all aware, Steve died before the date of your wedding, his will states: 'To Joseph Carlton and his wife, the former Melissa Pienta Tomlinson.'

"So, I'll need your name right next to Joe's," he instructed, now directing his eyes and his voice toward a slightly bewildered Melissa. "In the same eight places, I believe."

Melissa always had a great deal more respect for those businessmen who talked directly to her while she was in Joe's company. Too many others seemed to think, chauvinistically, that Joe's consent was needed before a decision by her became final. Almost immediately, Butler grew in her esteem.

"You see," Butler continued, almost as an afterthought, "Steve changed this will of his not too long ago. It was strange that he wanted to make this one, small addition—leaving the house to Joe and Melissa instead of just to Joe.

"I told him it wouldn't be necessary. After all, he had informed me long ago that you two were going to get married. Either way, the house would be community property. So I didn't see what difference it would make. However, Steve insisted. And even though, technically, you two weren't married at the time he changed his will, Steve assured me that your marriage was inevitable."

"Tell me," Melissa interjected. "When exactly was it that Uncle Steve decided to change this will?"

"The date was March the twenty-first."

Melissa and Joe looked into each other's eyes right away, as if on cue. March the twenty-first was smack in the middle of the period during which they'd had no intention of getting married. At about that time, they were semi-officially an estranged couple. In fact, one day earlier, on March the twentieth, Melissa had visited Uncle Steve for lunch. That was the occasion when he had given her his advice to "go down to Islamorada and claim your man."

Obviously, with this will of his as a vehicle, Uncle Steve was playing his own brand of a sure thing. For if Melissa and Joe had drifted apart, Uncle Steve's ultimate death might eventually have served to bring them back together.

In effect, how could a separated Melissa and Joe fail to consider the prospect of meeting with each other at least once, socially, to discuss how they would approach their dilemma?

After all, a house left jointly to two unmarried people who are supposed to be married is not an everyday problem that can be solved by a solitary phone call.

The will would demand that they meet, and Uncle Steve knew all too well the power that could explode from one spark of a renewed relationship between two former lovers.

"He was playing his last card," Joe commented. "It was an ace that he never needed."

"That was him, all right," Melissa concluded, her eyes meeting Joe's knowing smile. "Good old Uncle Steve. If things went wrong, you could always depend on him to produce a winning move."

Afterword

JOE AVENICK

I worked for James A. Michener during a five-year period in the 1970s. Thirty years after that I was outed as one of his ghostwriters—in Stephen J. May's 2005 biography of Michener, titled *Michener: A Writer's Journey*.

May revealed my role as a ghostwriter for sections of Michener's books *Sports in America* and *Chesapeake*.

I also found that I wasn't alone. May likewise highlighted the ghostwriting of Errol Uys, who wrote a good deal of Michener's *The Covenant* and other works. I never knew of Uys's existence until May interviewed me for his biography in 2003. Uys and I have since compared notes, and it is highly likely that there was at least one other ghostwriter who assisted Michener prior to our involvement and perhaps yet a fourth ghostwriter in the 1980s.

When I became aware of Michener's hiring of Uys, and considering the feature articles that I ghosted under Michener's name, it was then clear to me how Michener was able to "write" 70 mostly lengthy books and 398 magazine articles during his lifetime.

I first met Michener in 1973. Michener and his free-spending friend from Philadelphia, Edward Piszek, co-founder of Mrs. Paul's Kitchens, were looking for someone with knowledge of sports to assist Michener with the forthcoming *Sports in America*. Piszek's hefty wallet had bankrolled a number of Michener projects.

Michener knew he would need help because of his lack of knowledge about a number of sports, particularly football, golf, and track and field. The background I possessed as a newspaper sportswriter and columnist sealed our deal.

My first duties were to begin research for *Sports in America* and also to read the proof pages for Michener's novel *Centennial*, which he had just finished writing.

After completing the bulk of the sports research, I then wrote the first draft for most of the *Sports in America* chapters, save those few that were mostly Michener's recollections, theories, and recommendations. While Michener edited my first draft, I ghostwrote several magazine articles that appeared under his name in *The Saturday Evening Post* and in *Reader's Digest*.

After we finished *Sports in America*, I continued to work for Michener on his next book, *Chesapeake*. The work varied slightly on this project. Michener and I spent several months in St. Michaels, Maryland, trying to outline the work, selecting fictional names, and smoothing the plot. I then completed the detailed outline while Michener traveled about Maryland researching the sections that needed shoring up.

During my time in his employ, Michener and I would travel together throughout the United States, to Europe, and to the Middle East. Michener also visited me in Islamorada, the Florida Keys, where I introduced him to Melissa (Missy) DeMaio, an always-cheerful business-woman who had no idea of his background and who had never read any of his books. Michener and DeMaio soon began a love affair—with Michener's visits to the Keys then increasing exponentially.

I left Michener's employ in 1978 for other interests, but we remained friends for the next 19 years, until Michener died in October of 1997.

Michener's relationship with DeMaio inspired him to write *Matecumbe* (the word "Matecumbe" refers to two of the four islands that comprise Islamorada: Upper Matecumbe and Lower Matecumbe). He first showed me a rough draft sometime in the late 1970s, asking me for an opinion. Michener's first version of *Matecumbe* had a single female lead by the name of Melissa and was in the form of a three-act play, something he had never before attempted. He told me he had always admired playwright Arthur Miller and was also intrigued by the fact that Ernest Hemingway wrote only one play during his lifetime, *The Fifth Column*.

In the second version of *Matecumbe* that Michener showed me, about a year later, he had transformed it into a novella. I told him, frankly, that the longish dialogue gave it the feeling of a play but that it still worked as a novella.

Michener wanted Random House, his publisher, to print *Matecumbe*. But Michener's Random House editor, Albert Erskine, did not. Erskine told Michener he feared that *Matecumbe* was "just a love story," much like Michener's earlier novella, *Sayonara*, and that Michener shouldn't compromise his burgeoning reputation as a historical novelist.

Erskine told Michener that Random House CEO Tony Wimpfheimer also disliked the prospect of publishing *Matecumbe* and that Michener should stick with those long, thoroughly researched books that dealt with the history of Hawaii, Spain, Colorado, and the like. (A number of years later, I tracked down Wimpfheimer, who had retired and was living in Purchase, New York. Wimpfheimer told me that the decision to scuttle *Matecumbe* was entirely Erskine's decision.)

Amazingly, Erskine also tried to steer Michener away from writing any more small books similar to *Tales of the South Pacific*, which won Michener a Pulitzer Prize and was the basis for the long-running musical "South Pacific."

"Erskine forced me to look at the bottom line," Michener remembered. "Heavyweight books like *Hawaii* and *Centennial* made chunks of money."

Although he relented to Erskine, Michener still held hope that Random House would one day consent to publish *Matecumbe*. He was convinced that this novella was even better than *Sayonara*, also a story of two love affairs, which had become a best-seller as well as an Academy Award winning motion picture starring Marlon Brando.

I met with Michener sporadically through the early 1980s. And even though he and DeMaio had then split, he was still reworking *Matecumbe*.

Michener told me that he had been on the peer review list in the early 1950s for Ernest Hemingway's novella, *The Old Man and the Sea*, which later won Hemingway both the Pulitzer Prize and the Nobel Prize for Literature (1954). This peer review is described by Michener in a 38-page introduction he wrote for a later edition of Hemingway's *The Dangerous Summer*.

After reading the proofs, Michener was overwhelmed with the allegories and symbolism of *The Old Man and the Sea*. He would try, Michener said, to put the same elements into *Matecumbe*.

"Hemingway told a simple story of a fisherman that seemed to be a saccharine treatment at first reading," Michener said. "Instead of a fisherman, I finally found my vehicle—two divorced women. In *Matecumbe*, I want to hide the deeper thoughts between the lines of the two love stories. I need *Matecumbe* to exhale slowly all of the symbols and allegories."

During his fine-tuning of rewrites, Michener peppered me for suggestions such as "give me a good name for a cat" (Puff) or "what do people do when they visit the Islamorada Hurricane Monument?" (gaze in awe). He also decided to scrap one of his favorite devices—a geological history preface that for *Matecumbe* would have discussed the evolution of topography in the Florida Keys beginning with the Pleistocene epoch. "Too cumbersome for this book," he concluded.

In 1974, I had introduced Michener to my uncle, Stefan, whom he subsequently used as one of the gamblers ("The Pole") in *Sports in America*. I suspect that Michener was picturing Stefan while he rewrote an enhanced role for the Solomon-like Uncle Steve character in *Matecumbe*.

Eventually, Michener told me that there was no longer any chance of his convincing Random House to publish *Matecumbe*. He then gave me the manuscript outright, telling me that I could rewrite it if I wanted. Michener had sent me several letters indicating that he had gifted the manuscript to me, including one letter in which he specifically noted that he was giving me the copyright to *Matecumbe* as well as to other short pieces of nonfiction that he had written over the years.

This element of largesse was typical of Michener. To colleges and universities he gave millions of dollars. Friends and acquaintances rarely received money. Instead, he would give them personalized notes; handwritten poems; autographed books; and cooked hams at Christmas. Fellow ghostwriter Uys recalled the holiday goose that Michener gave him one year. It was inedible, though, being full of shot.

I often asked myself why Michener gave me the *Matecumbe* manuscript. It would be flattering to think he considered me the son he never had, but it was probably due more to trust. Most notable, I knew of his extramarital affair with DeMaio. His secretary/travel agent also knew (receipts from a trip to the Isle of Capri), and she received checks from Michener on a regular basis. I asked for nothing.

To the best of my memory, sometime in 1983 or 1984, Michener sent me some final paragraphs that he said should be inserted into the manuscript. From that point through this initial publication of *Matecumbe*, I never changed one word.* The more I read *Matecumbe*, the more I was certain it could not be improved—by me or by anyone. To me, reading it was like watching the film *Harold and Maude*. Every time I saw it, I recognized something new.

While Michener was alive, I did nothing with the *Matecumbe* manuscript. After his death, I made a few informal inquiries to publishing houses, but there was only mild interest. One acquisitions editor commented that "few people under fifty years of age have heard of Michener."

Then, about a decade ago, while I was working for literary agent E. Sidney Porcelain, my curiosity bested me. One of my duties was to circulate sections of manuscripts that Porcelain had received from writers. I would regularly solicit opinions from other writers and editors that I respected, helping Porcelain to decide whether to represent these authors. Occasionally, I would send out copies of pages from *Matecumbe* to these reviewers, not telling them that Michener was the author. About half of my reviewers raved over *Matecumbe*, while the others were indifferent. One reviewer, who missed the point of the character development entirely, wrote a lengthy expansion of two Michener pages, declaring that "the Carlton character needs more depth."

In the summer of 2005 I was in discussions with the editors at the University Press of Florida concerning a book I proposed on the history of celebrities in the Florida Keys. The editors then approached me about the *Matecumbe* manuscript after reading about it in May's biography of Michener.

The first thing I explained to them was that this Michener novella may be light on pages, but it is far from a simple book.

---

* The publisher has corrected typographical and compositional errors and errors of fact or meaning.

In *Matecumbe*, the symbols and allegories that fill this apparently simple dual love story would require a trilogy to explain. Michener himself admitted that most of his loyal readers would like it but would probably fail to appreciate all facets of *Matecumbe* and would assume that it was merely a tale of two love relationships.

Sage advice would be that readers need to think as they read and that they should weigh the possible alternate/hidden meanings in *Matecumbe*. Specifically, they should ponder the recurring mention of the color blue as it concerns both Melissa and Mary Ann; the "why" behind the Reynolds character falling in love with Mary Ann; the old woman in the cemetery; the white cat, Coke; Carlton's fear of hurricanes; the number of seeds in a watermelon; and especially the dialogue of the Uncle Steve character. If Francis Scott Key Fitzgerald can be commended for his words between the words in *The Great Gatsby* and his sharp social insight through symbolism, so, too, can Michener. As the Roman poet Horace stated, he "built a monument more lasting than bronze."

Overall, *Matecumbe* is similar in structure and plot coursing to several of Michener's previous works. Yet, it is also different, having a cutting edge that makes Michener's characters come off as less straight-laced and less righteous.

Any critic who reads *Matecumbe* and concludes that it is "not exactly Michener" is probably right. It is, in reality, "Michener Plus." I believe that his relationship with DeMaio caused this change. Prior to meeting DeMaio, Michener had the archetypical aloof Quaker personality. Afterward, he was more open, gregarious, and inquisitive. This alteration in his psyche is also evident in other books he wrote post-1984 and in the characters he created post-DeMaio. If we concede that Melissa (Missy) DeMaio was the real-life inspiration for the Melissa character in *Matecumbe*, then it is obvious that DeMaio was also the inspiration for the "Melissa (Missy) Peckham" in Michener's 1988 novel, *Alaska*. It is also a given that "Peckham" is unlike any Michener character who appeared prior to his involvement with DeMaio.

It should be noted, for proper context, that Michener's gift to me of the *Matecumbe* manuscript did not occur in a vacuum. Throughout the years, Michener also gave me a number of short works that he wrote and then decided not to have published—for various reasons.

According to Michener, the ten short features on Russia, based on his visit there in 1974, were "mere reflections on conditions in the Soviet Union at that time." Michener added that "the Russian stories can't really be packaged successfully to address a viable target audience of readers."

The series of twelve connected stories he wrote about life in Florida were not mere reflections but were cultural analyses of the people in that state. Michener worried, though, that these Florida stories would be received as politically incorrect and might infuriate some readers. Criticizing and making enemies of northern Florida rednecks, Cubans, and Haitians doesn't leave room for many friends. (For example, one story is titled *When the Last Real American Leaves Miami*.) Thus, the mothballs.

Finally, his haiku poems, about historical figures and locations in America, were scrapped in favor of his book of sonnets, which was published shortly before he died.

One other gift from Michener was an apparently innocuous two-page outline.

I had told Michener that I was working on a novel about racism in the United States, set in Florida and New York. To date, I am still engaged in creating this work of fiction, which attempts to define the sensibilities of our age.

When I explained that several of my characters would be neo-Nazis pitched against the Mafia, and that I was debating how to organize and outline my novel, Michener remembered an outline he had written for a book that he never wrote about Austria in World War I.

"Use this if you want," Michener told me, referring to his outline. "I boosted structure guidelines from Honoré de Balzac and others. This outline will show you one way that you can intersperse events to justify your characters' acts, whether you write about Austria, China, heaven, or hell. Good luck with it."

I then promised Michener that I would continue to write my racism novel.

Sometime in the near future, I'll know whether Michener's outline works.

If what I produce is as good as *Matecumbe*, I'll be satisfied.

James A. Michener (1907–1997) won the Pulitzer Prize for Fiction in 1948 for his *Tales of the South Pacific* and was awarded the Presidential Medal of Freedom in 1977. He was the author of nearly forty books including *Centennial* (1974), *Texas* (1985), and *Alaska* (1988). His novels have sold in excess of seventy-five million copies worldwide.